NORSE MYTHS

A VIKING GRAPHIC NOVEL

THE DEATH OF BALDUR

by LOUISE SIMONSON and EDUARDO GARCIA

STONE ARCH BOOKS

a capstone imprint

Norse Myths is published by Stone Arch Books
A Capstone Imprint
1710 Roe Crest Drive
North Mankato, Minnesota 56003
www.mycapstone.com

Cataloging-in-Publication Data is available at the Library of Congress website.
ISBN: 978-1-4965-3488-0 (hardcover)
ISBN: 978-1-4965-3492-7 (paperback)
ISBN: 978-1-4965-3496-5 (eBook PDF)

Summary: Baldur, Odin's greatest son, is a leader of men and loved by all. So when a prophecy is made that the end of the world, Ragnarök, the Twilight of the Gods, will occur when Baldur dies, Odin imprisons all those who might be involved in the death of his beloved son. But fate is fate. Baldur will die—the only question is how. And the result will be the beginning of the end for all of creation.

Editor: Aaron Sautter
Designer: Kristi Carlson
Production Specialist: Laura Manthe

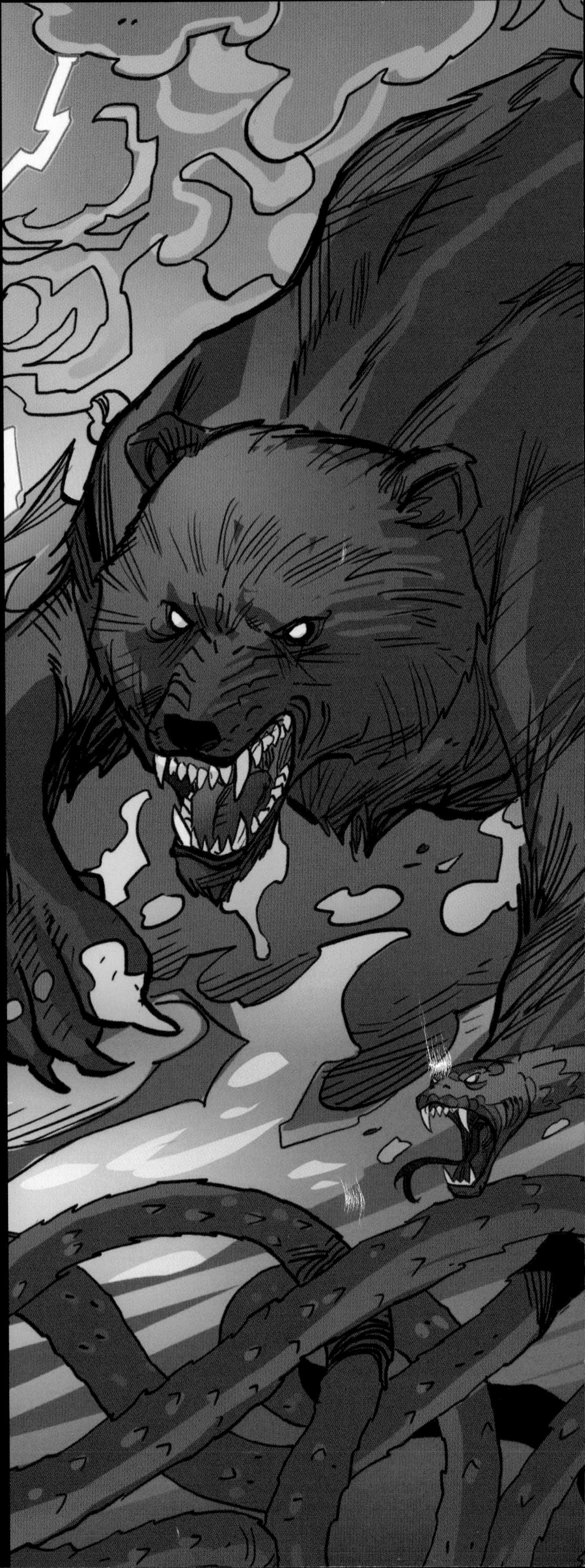

Printed in the United States of America.
009624F16

TABLE OF CONTENTS

A TERRIBLE PROPHECY

The Norse people, or Vikings, lived in a cold and harsh world. They survived mostly by hunting, fishing, trading, and raiding their neighbors. To help understand their world, the Vikings created stories about powerful gods who controlled the world and everything in it.

According to Norse myths, the Norse gods, or Aesir, often behaved much like the Viking people. The gods were often beautiful, wise, and strong. But they could also be vain, weak, jealous, and foolish.

Odin, ruler of the Aesir, sought wisdom and knowledge from many sources. He even sacrificed one of his eyes to gain a clearer vision of the future. Odin's thirst for knowledge grew more desperate when he learned about the prophesied fate of the Aesir.

The death of Baldur, Odin's beloved son, would cause him great pain. But the All-Father knew that Baldur's murder would have much greater meaning. He knew that the evil act would be the first event of Ragnarök, and signal the beginning of the end of the Norse gods ...

THE FAMILY OF GODS

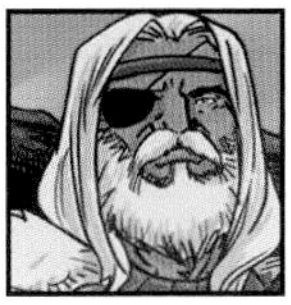

Odin—the All-Father, and ruler of the Norse gods, the Aesir. He is the husband of Frigg and has great knowledge and wisdom.

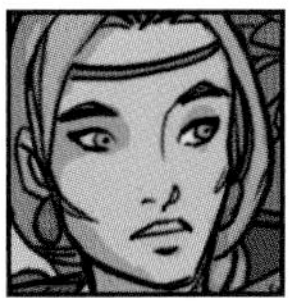

Frigg—Odin's wife and queen of the Aesir. She is the Norse goddess of marriage and a wise seeress and magician.

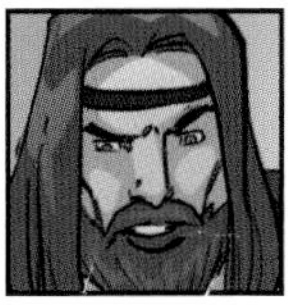

Thor—the Norse god of thunder. He is the strongest of the gods and Earth's protector. Easily angered, Thor can call lightning from the sky with his mighty war hammer, Mjölnir.

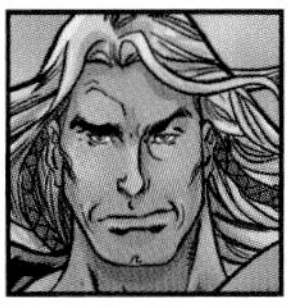

Baldur—the handsome god of light, and Odin's most beloved son. He was the favorite of all creatures and people of the Nine Worlds, except one.

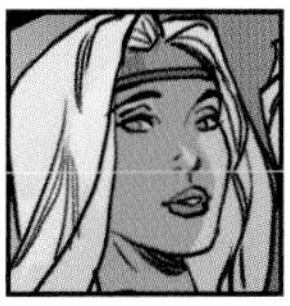

Nanna—Baldur's wife who dies of grief at her beloved husband's untimely death.

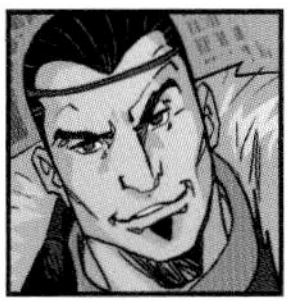

Loki—a giant and blood brother to the gods. A clever shape-shifter, Loki enjoys tricking the Norse gods. His jealousy of Baldur leads to actions that trigger the coming of Ragnarök.

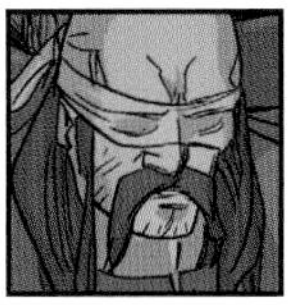

Hodur—the blind son of Odin. He is unable to participate in the Aesir's games and is easily fooled.

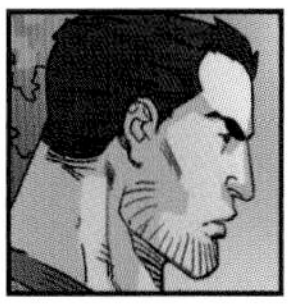

Hermod—the messenger of the gods, and a loyal son and servant of Odin.

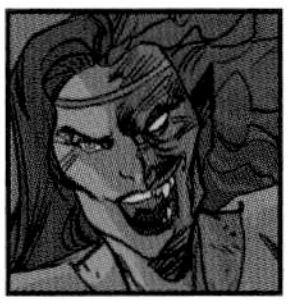

Hel—the hideous half-human, half-monster daughter of Loki who rules over the land of the dead.

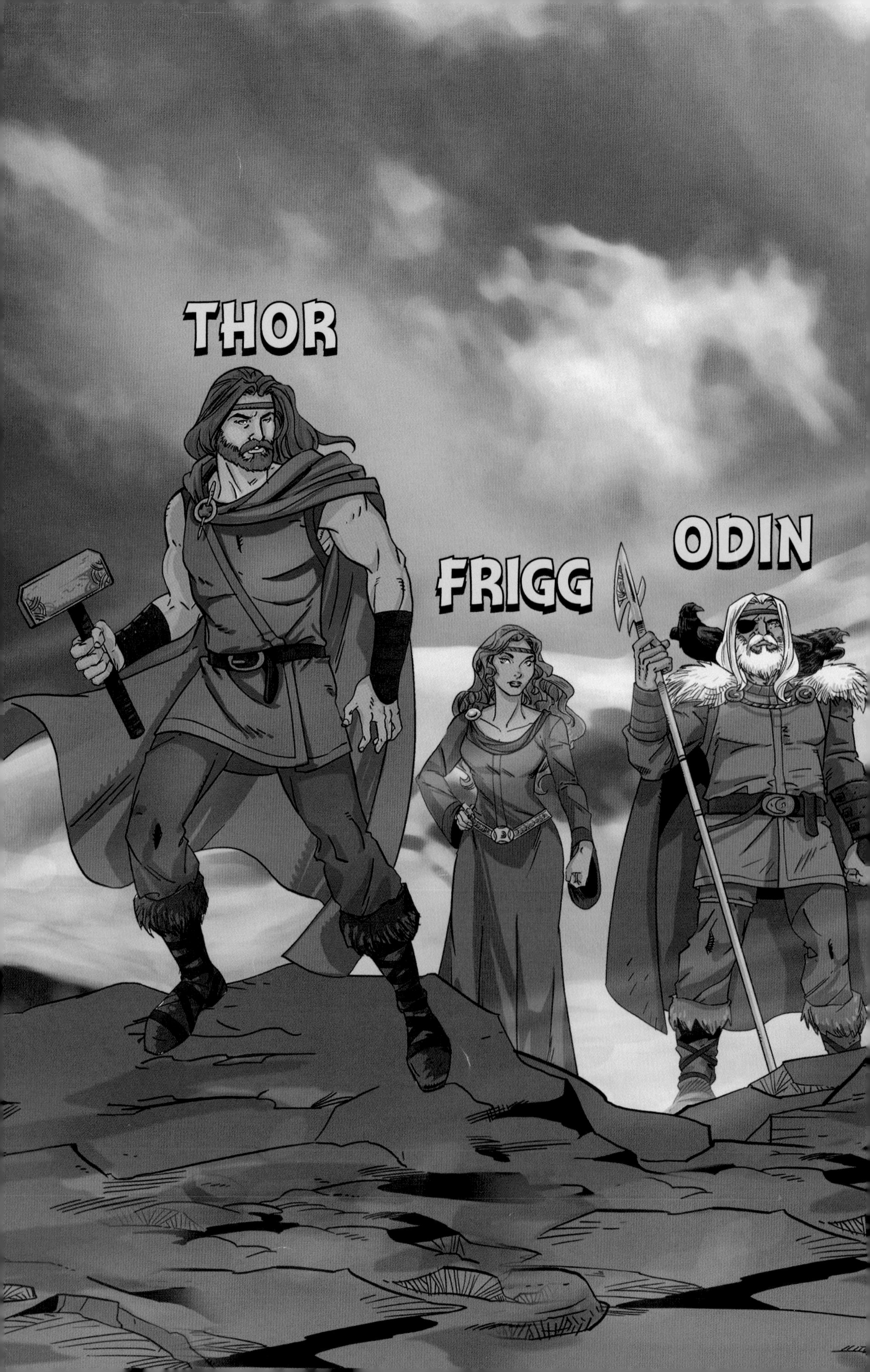
THOR
FRIGG
ODIN

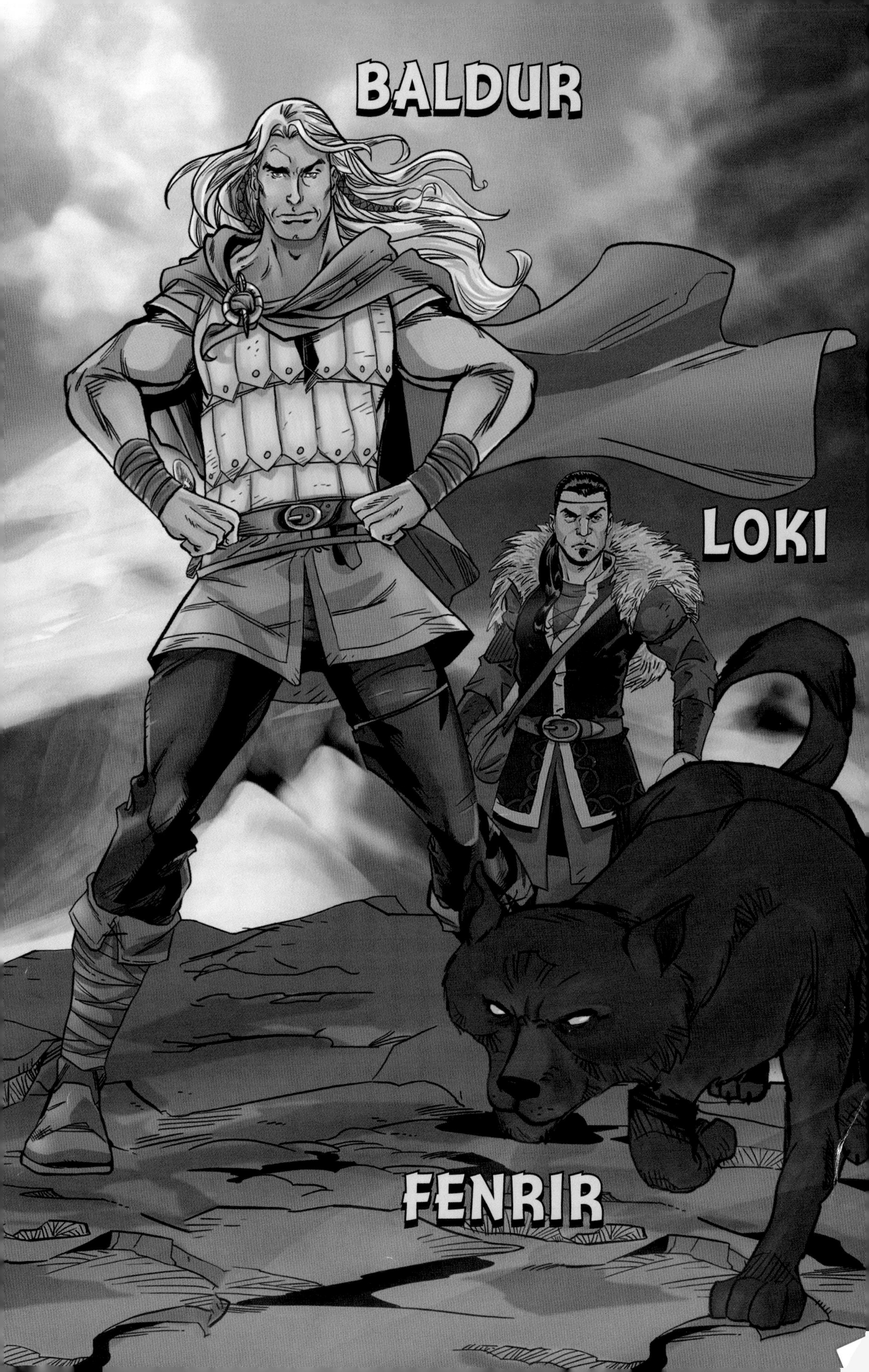
BALDUR
LOKI
FENRIR

CHAPTER 1
DREAMS AND NIGHTMARES

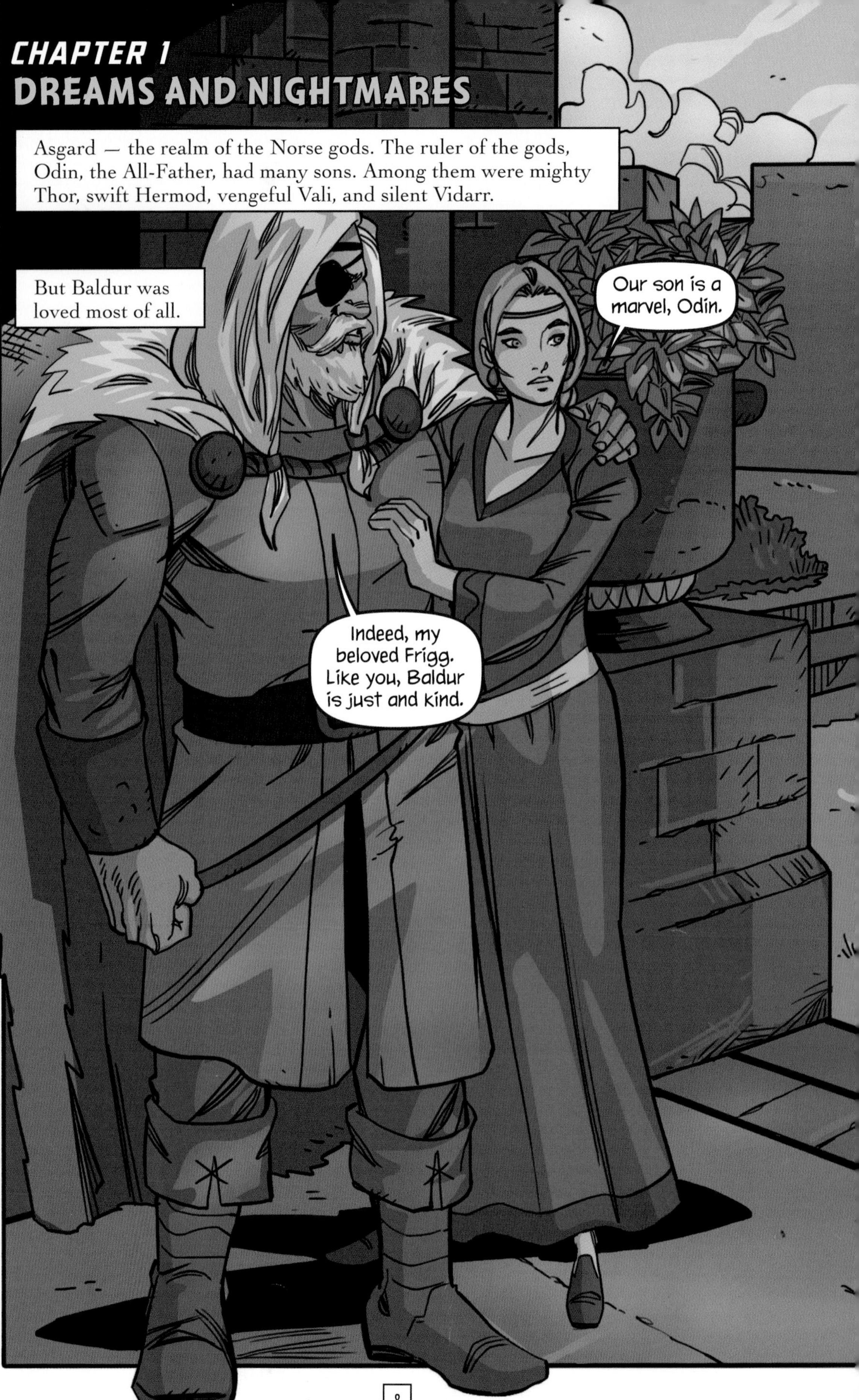
Asgard — the realm of the Norse gods. The ruler of the gods, Odin, the All-Father, had many sons. Among them were mighty Thor, swift Hermod, vengeful Vali, and silent Vidarr.
But Baldur was loved most of all.
Our son is a marvel, Odin.
Indeed, my beloved Frigg. Like you, Baldur is just and kind.

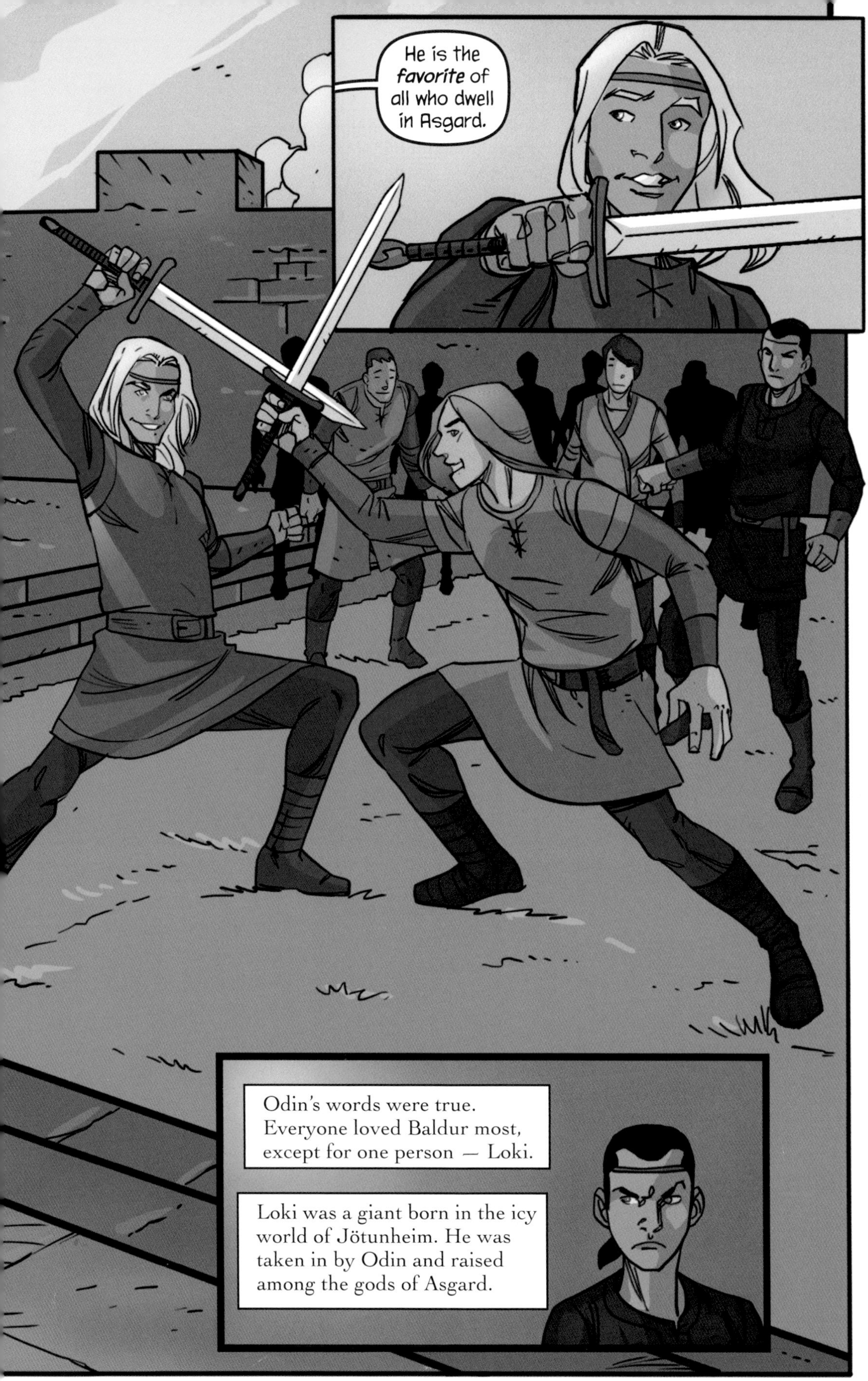
He is the *favorite* of all who dwell in Asgard.
Odin's words were true. Everyone loved Baldur most, except for one person — Loki.
Loki was a giant born in the icy world of Jötunheim. He was taken in by Odin and raised among the gods of Asgard.

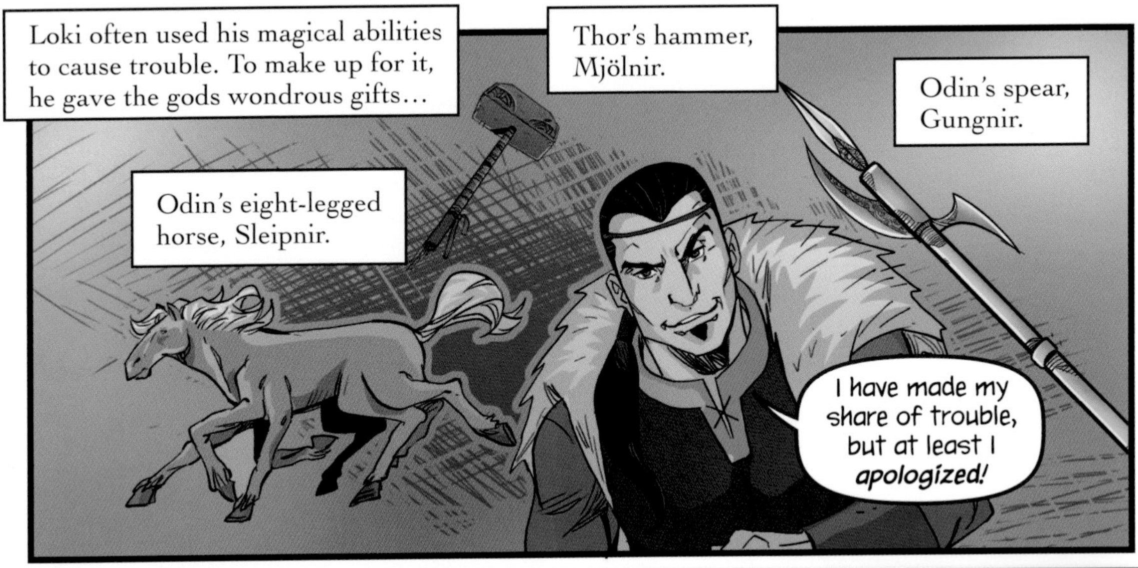
Loki often used his magical abilities to cause trouble. To make up for it, he gave the gods wondrous gifts…
Thor's hammer, Mjölnir.
Odin's spear, Gungnir.
Odin's eight-legged horse, Sleipnir.
I have made my share of trouble, but at least I *apologized!*

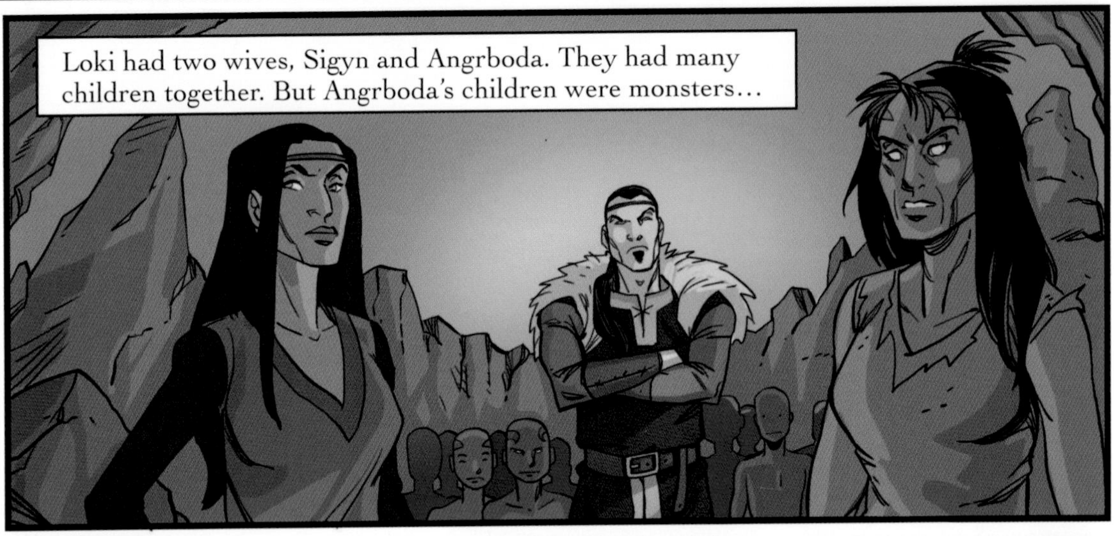
Loki had two wives, Sigyn and Angrboda. They had many children together. But Angrboda's children were monsters…

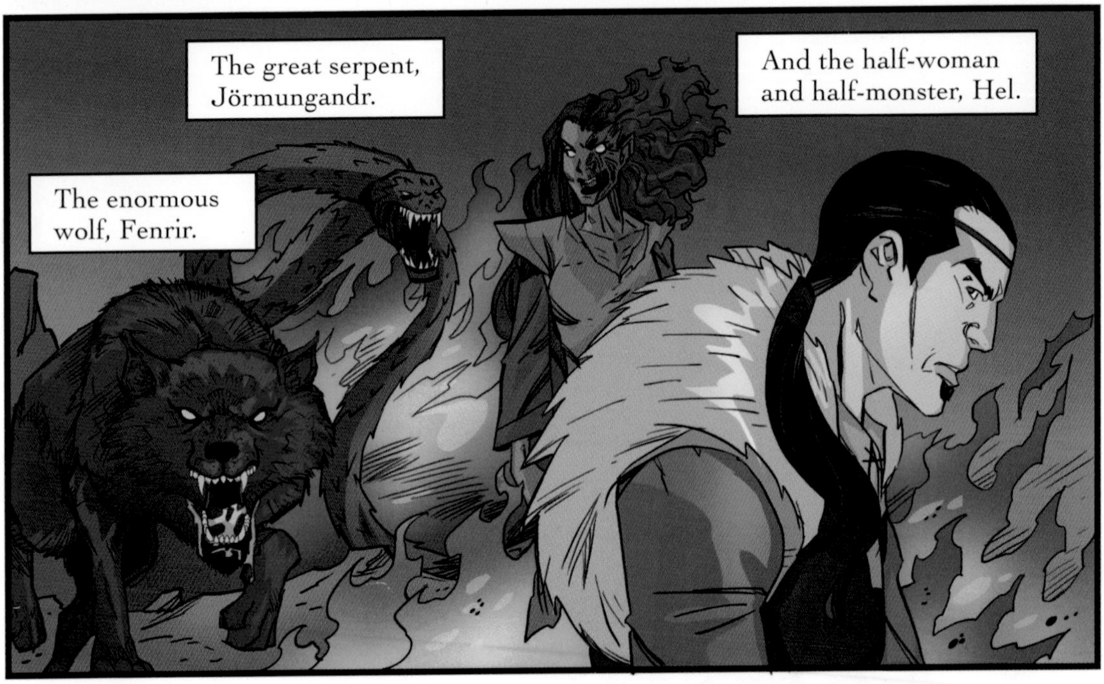
The great serpent, Jörmungandr.
And the half-woman and half-monster, Hel.
The enormous wolf, Fenrir.

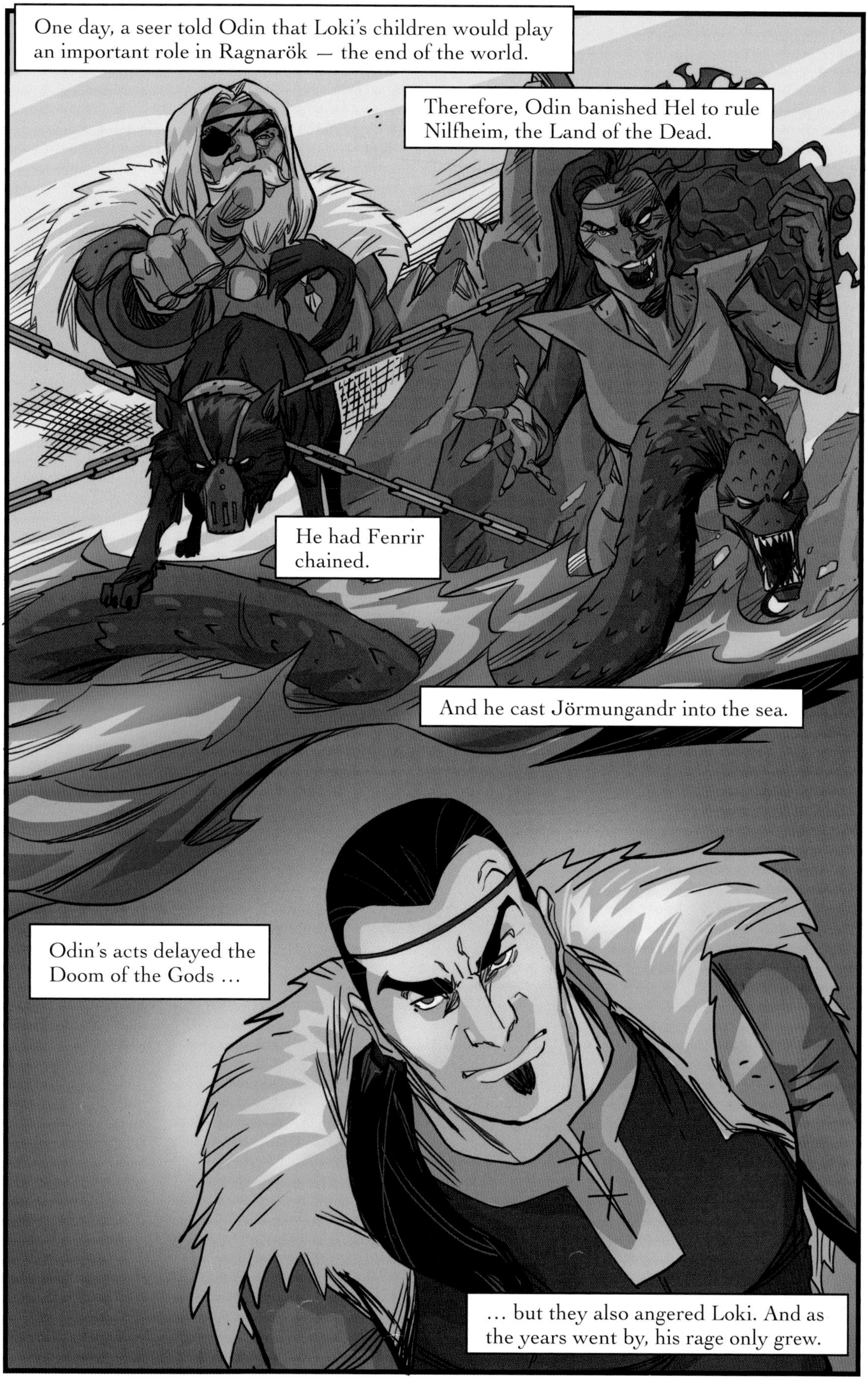
One day, a seer told Odin that Loki's children would play an important role in Ragnarök — the end of the world.
Therefore, Odin banished Hel to rule Nilfheim, the Land of the Dead.
He had Fenrir chained.
And he cast Jörmungandr into the sea.
Odin's acts delayed the Doom of the Gods …
… but they also angered Loki. And as the years went by, his rage only grew.

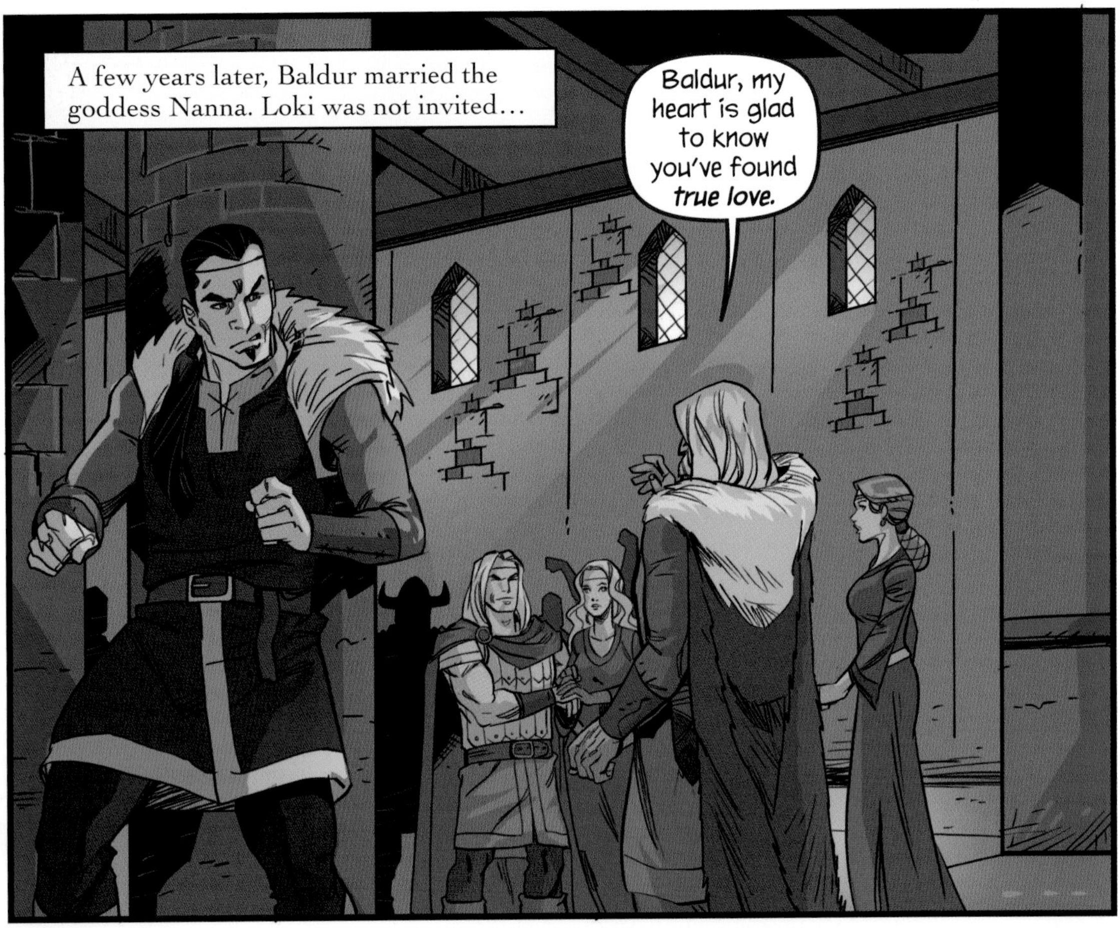
A few years later, Baldur married the goddess Nanna. Loki was not invited...
Baldur, my heart is glad to know you've found *true love.*

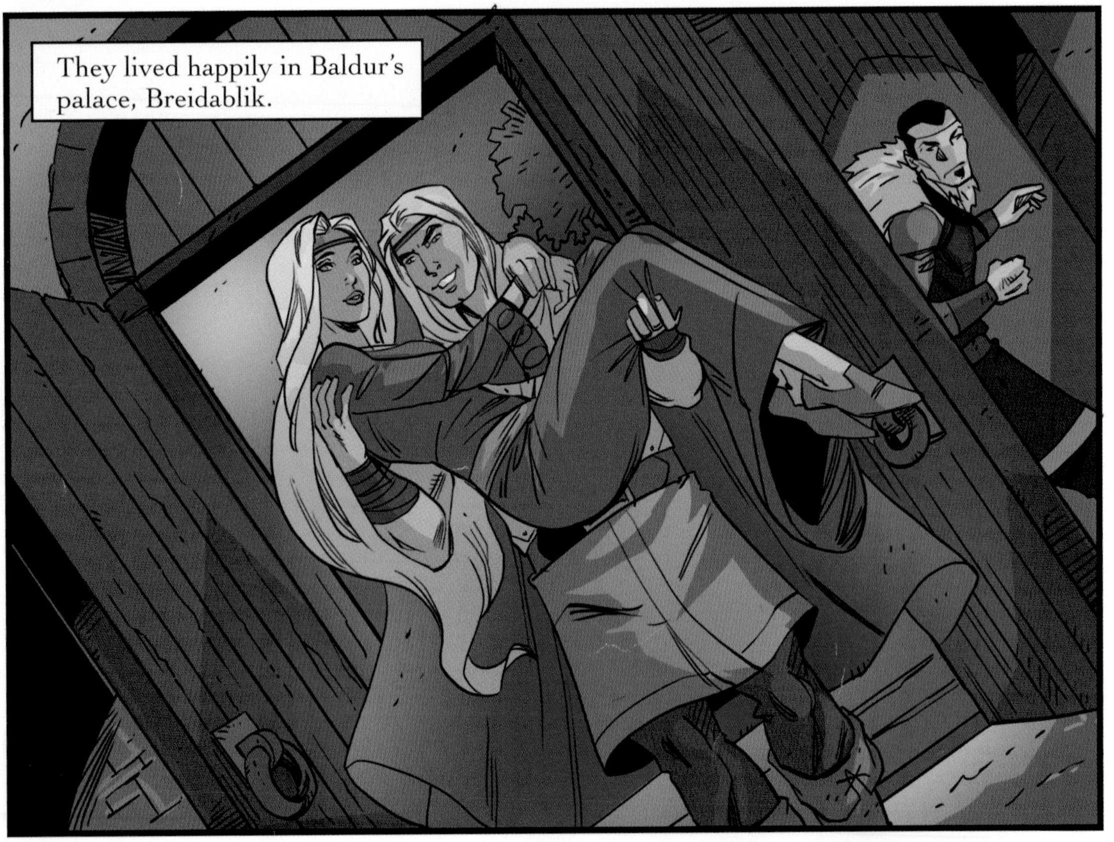
They lived happily in Baldur's palace, Breidablik.

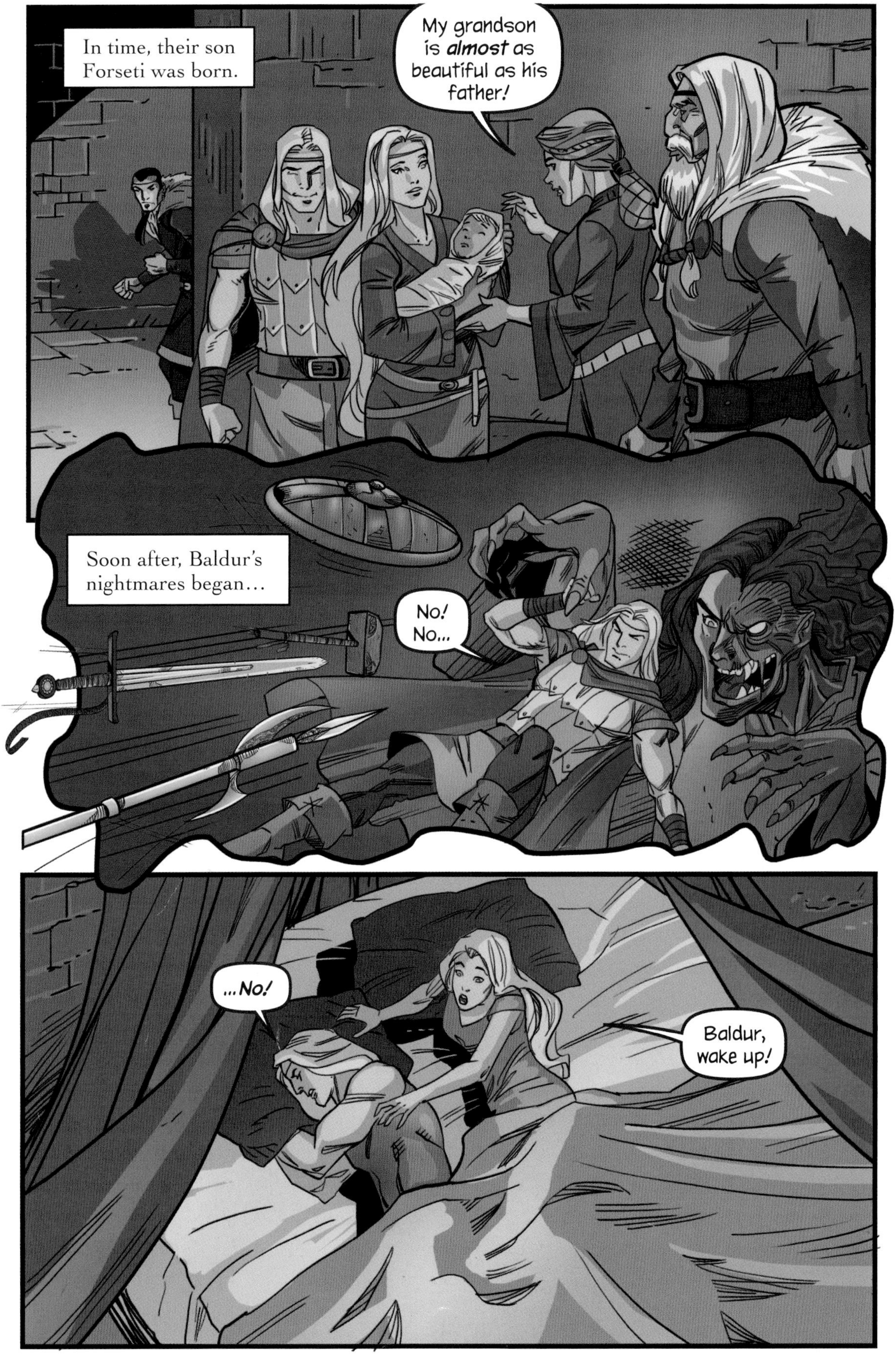
In time, their son Forseti was born.
My grandson is *almost* as beautiful as his father!
Soon after, Baldur's nightmares began…
No! No…
…No!
Baldur, wake up!

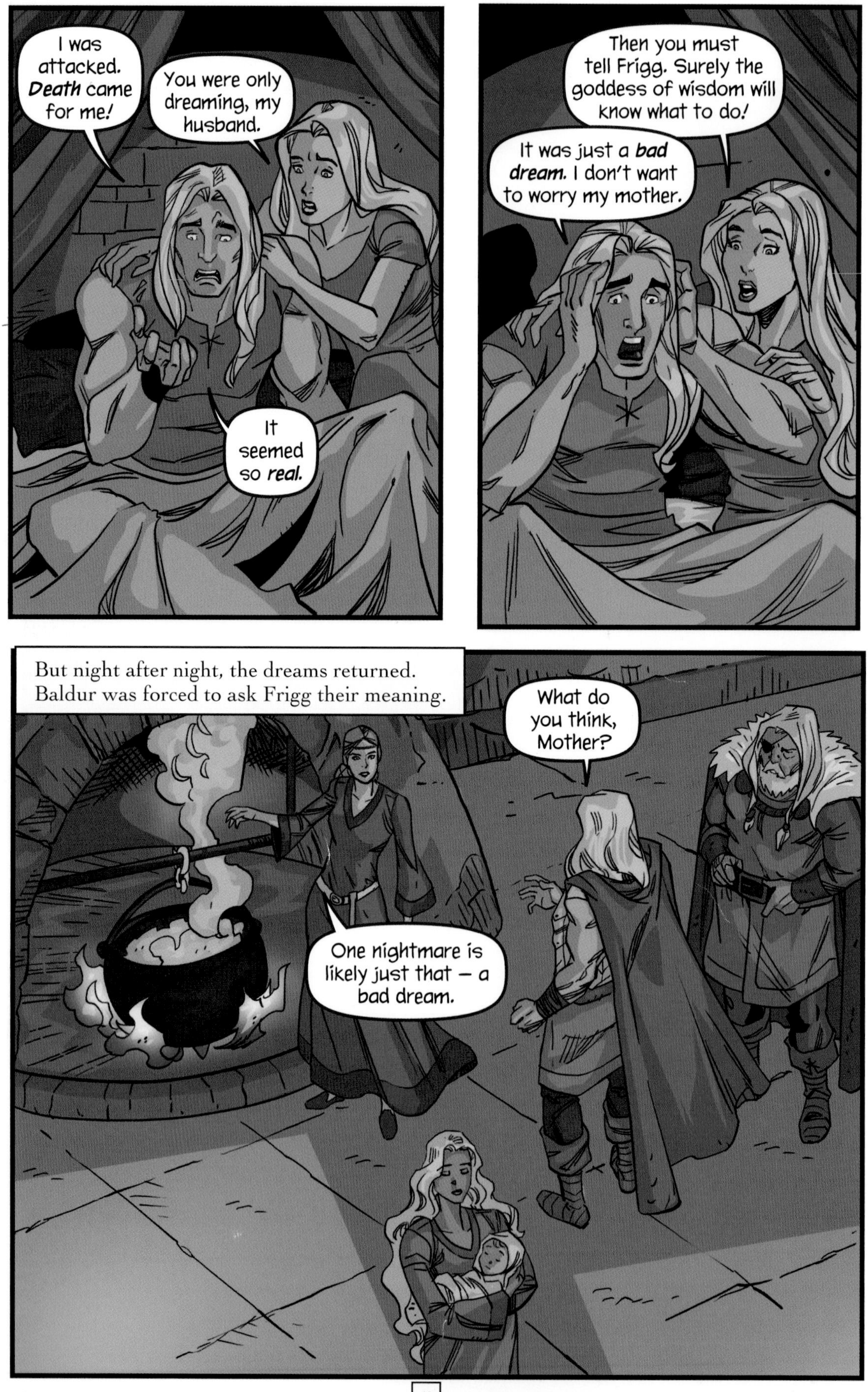
I was attacked. *Death* came for me!
You were only dreaming, my husband.
It seemed so *real.*
Then you must tell Frigg. Surely the goddess of wisdom will know what to do!
It was just a *bad dream.* I don't want to worry my mother.
But night after night, the dreams returned. Baldur was forced to ask Frigg their meaning.
What do you think, Mother?
One nightmare is likely just that — a bad dream.

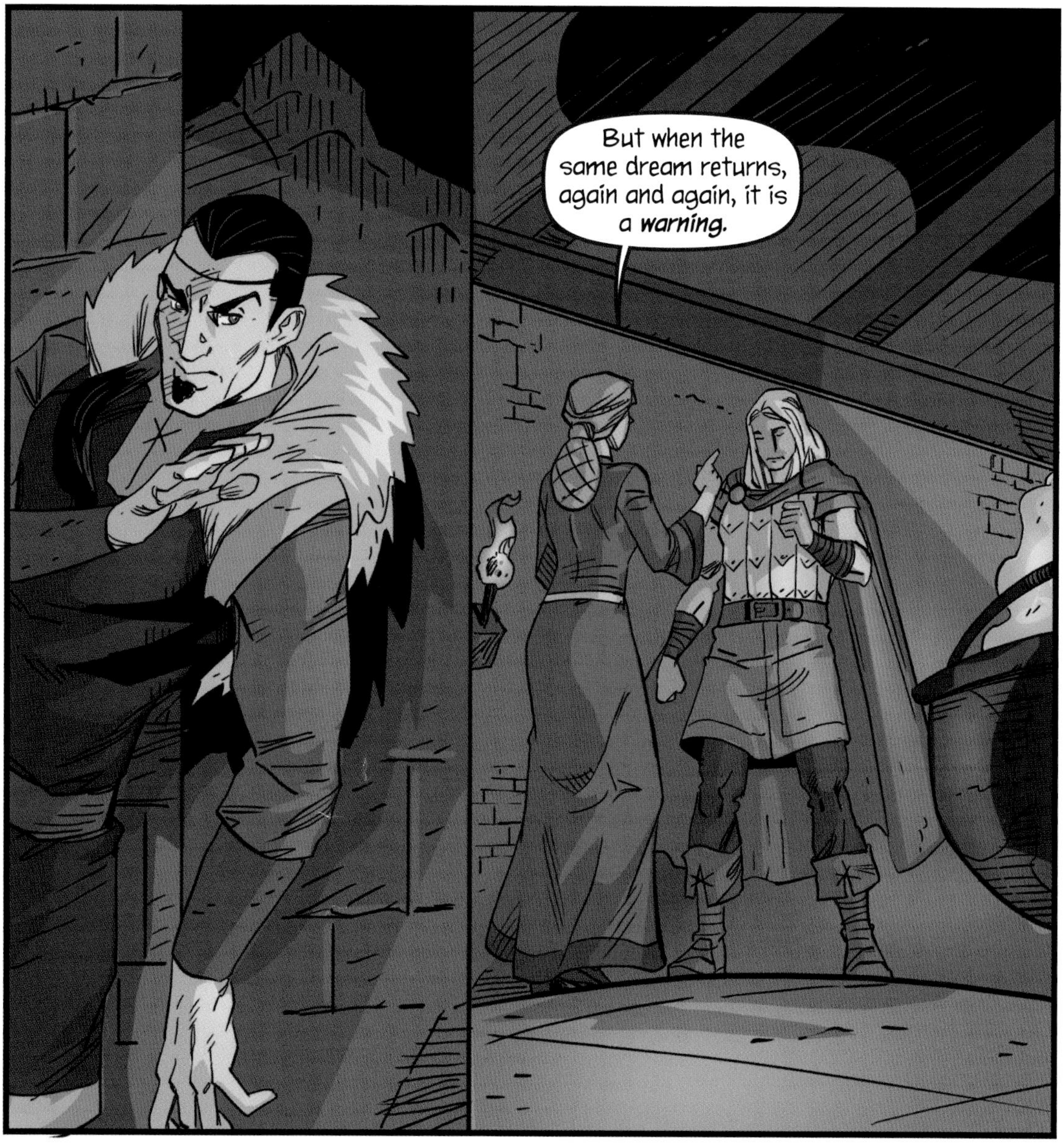
But when the same dream returns, again and again, it is a ***warning.***

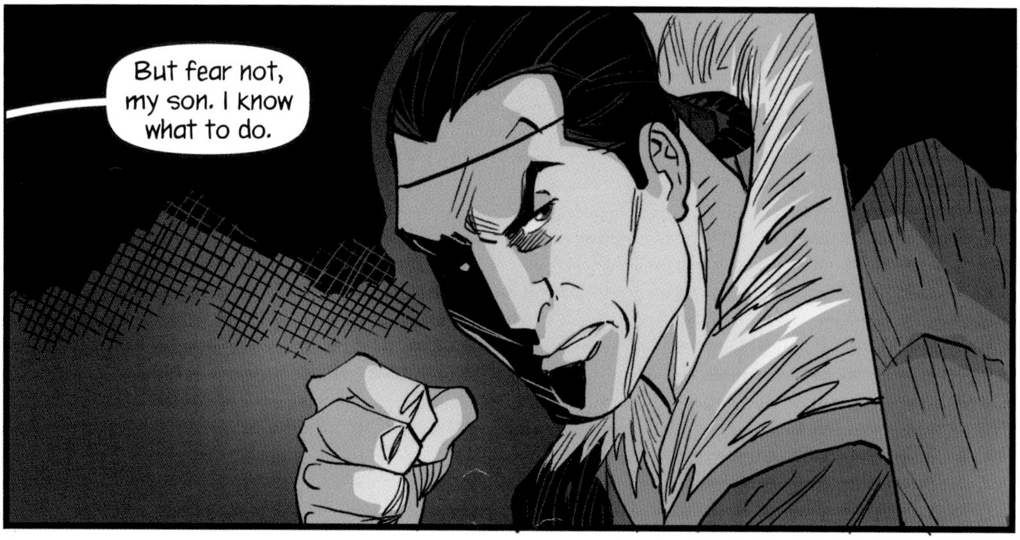
But fear not, my son. I know what to do.

CHAPTER 2
A MOTHER'S PROTECTION

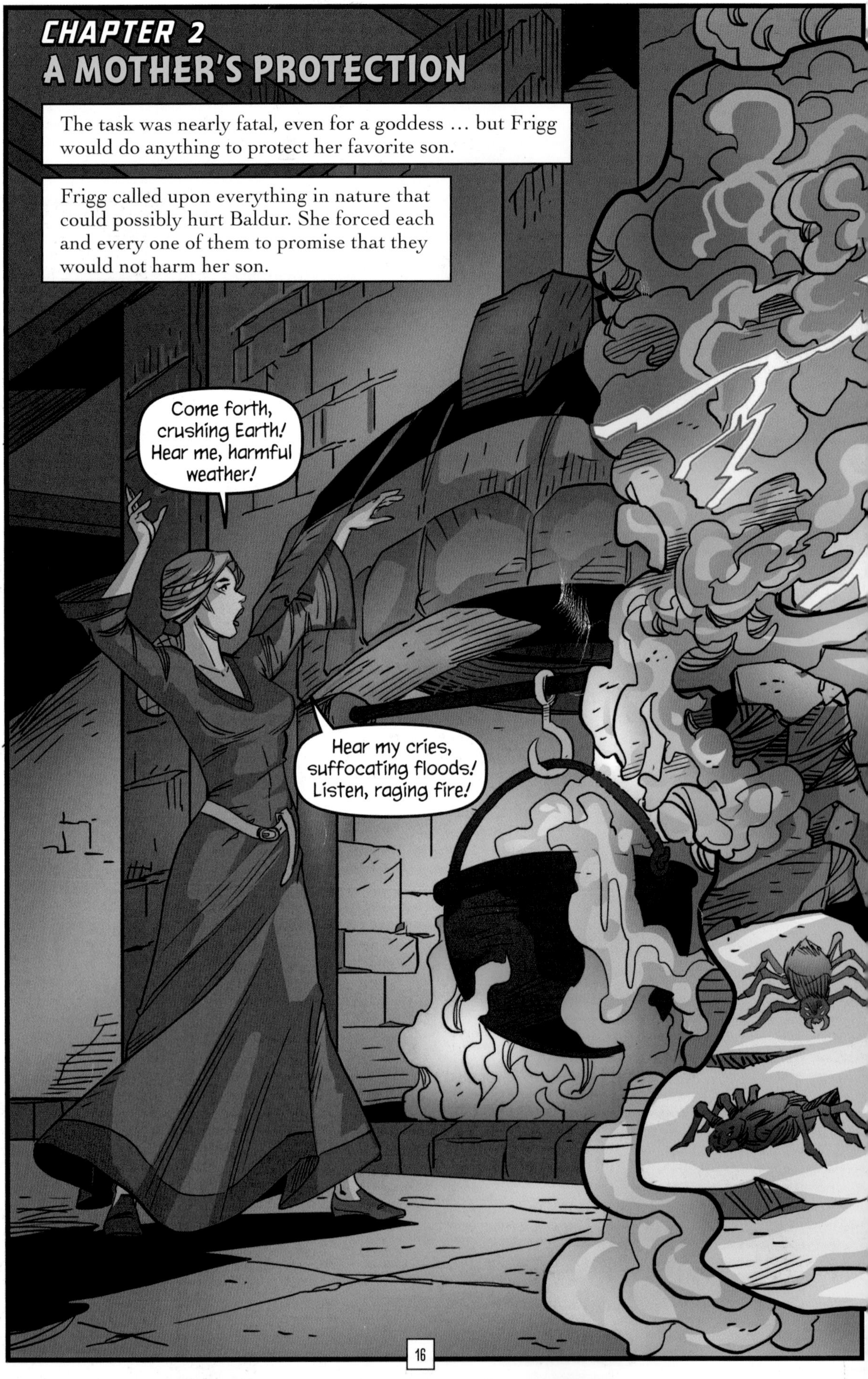
The task was nearly fatal, even for a goddess … but Frigg would do anything to protect her favorite son.
Frigg called upon everything in nature that could possibly hurt Baldur. She forced each and every one of them to promise that they would not harm her son.
Come forth, crushing Earth! Hear me, harmful weather!
Hear my cries, suffocating floods! Listen, raging fire!

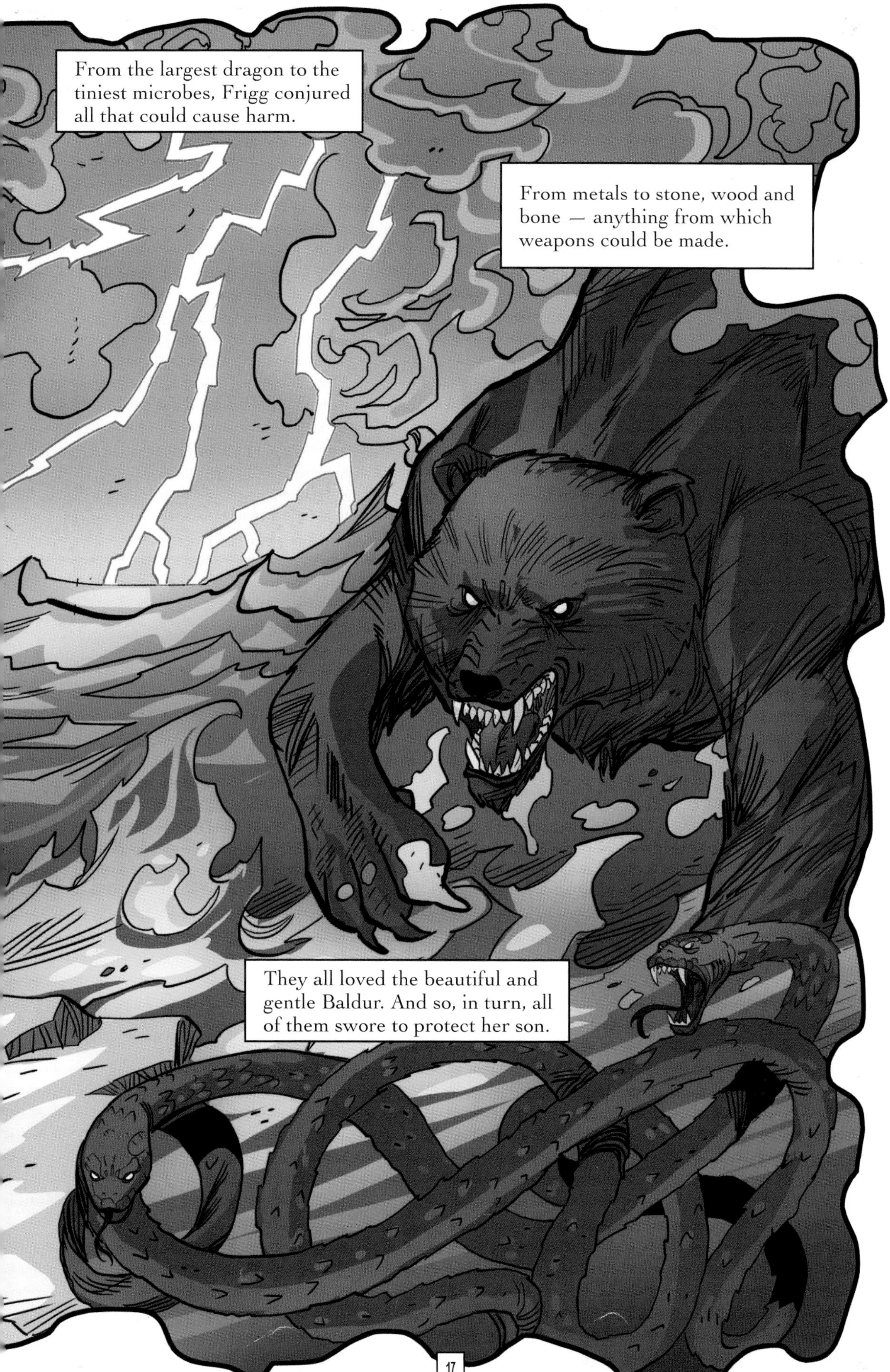
From the largest dragon to the tiniest microbes, Frigg conjured all that could cause harm.
From metals to stone, wood and bone — anything from which weapons could be made.
They all loved the beautiful and gentle Baldur. And so, in turn, all of them swore to protect her son.

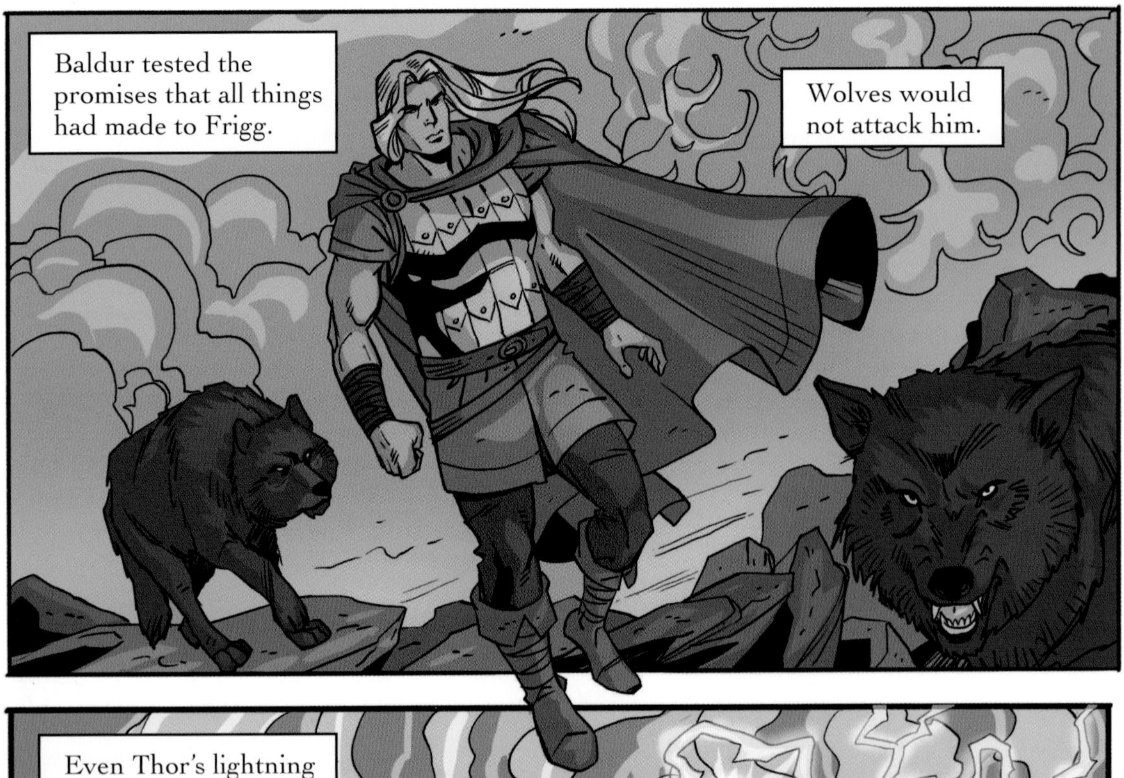
Baldur tested the promises that all things had made to Frigg.
Wolves would not attack him.

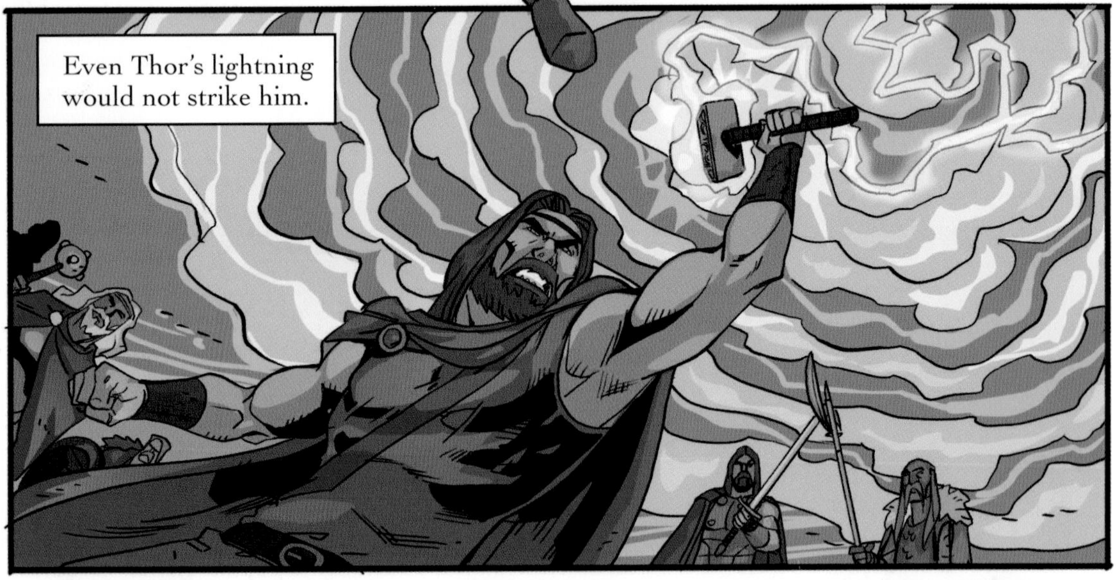
Even Thor's lightning would not strike him.

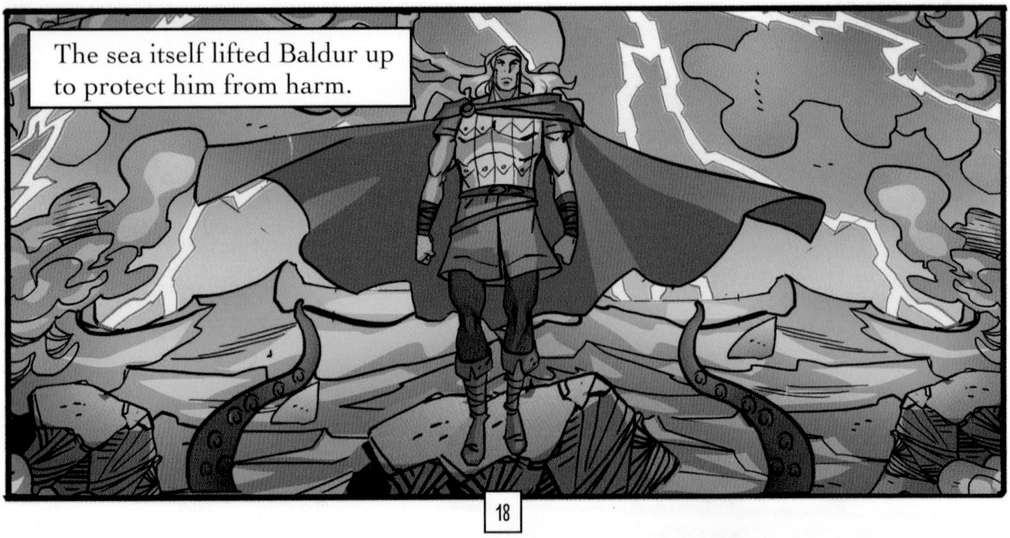
The sea itself lifted Baldur up to protect him from harm.

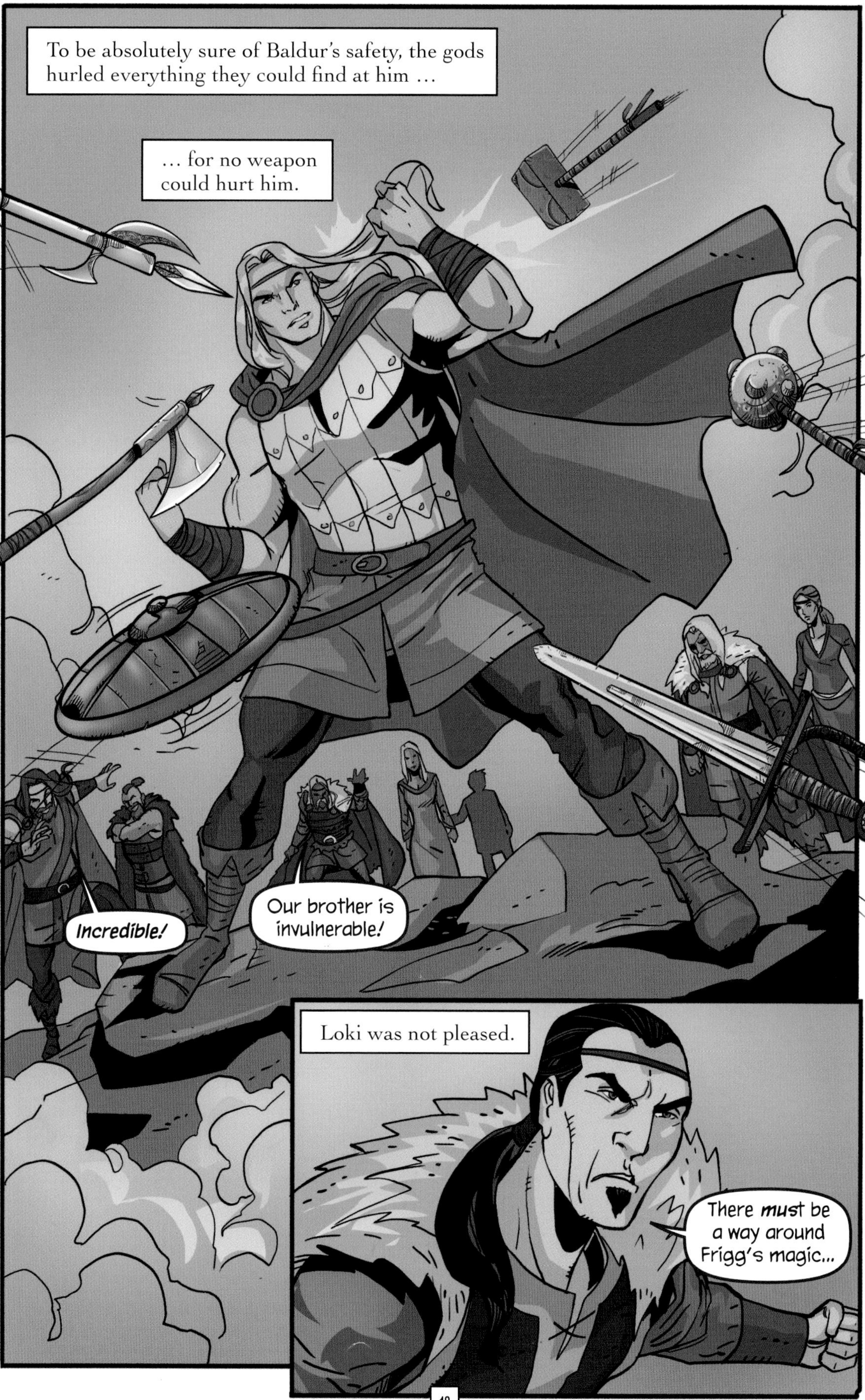
To be absolutely sure of Baldur's safety, the gods hurled everything they could find at him …
… for no weapon could hurt him.
Incredible!
Our brother is invulnerable!
Loki was not pleased.
There must be a way around Frigg's magic...

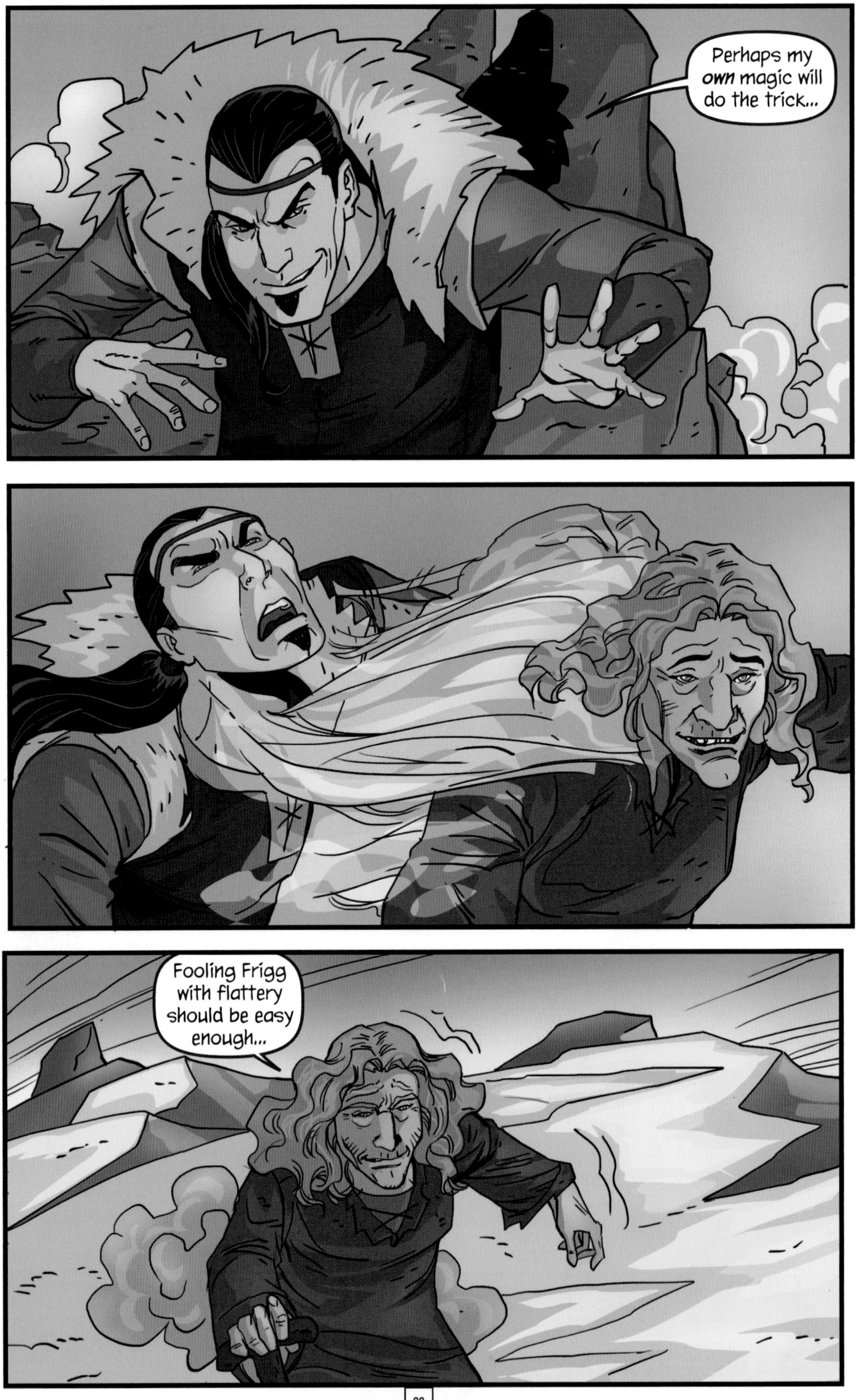
Perhaps my *own* magic will do the trick...
Fooling Frigg with flattery should be easy enough...

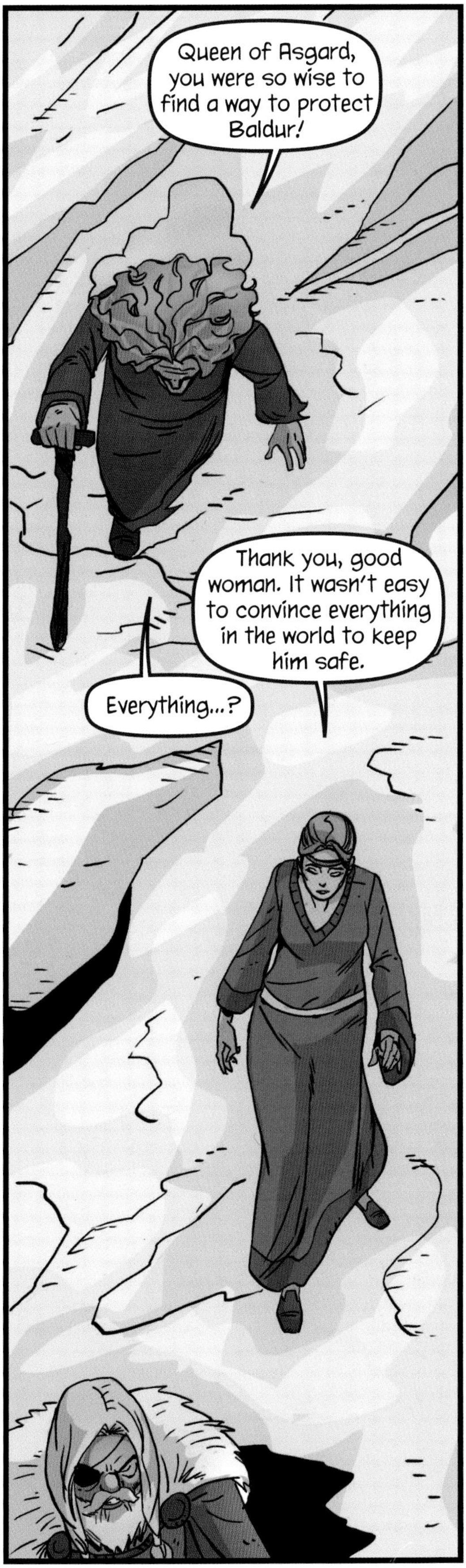
Queen of Asgard, you were so wise to find a way to protect Baldur!
Thank you, good woman. It wasn't easy to convince everything in the world to keep him safe.
Everything...?

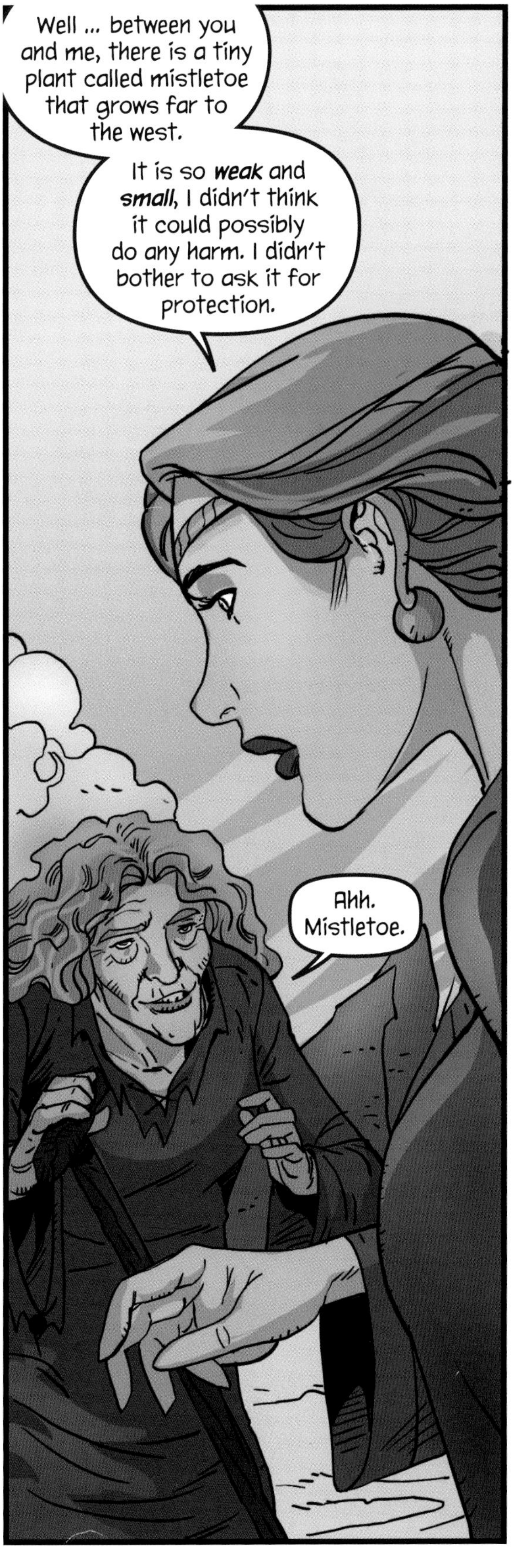
Well ... between you and me, there is a tiny plant called mistletoe that grows far to the west.
It is so ***weak*** and ***small***, I didn't think it could possibly do any harm. I didn't bother to ask it for protection.
Ahh. Mistletoe.

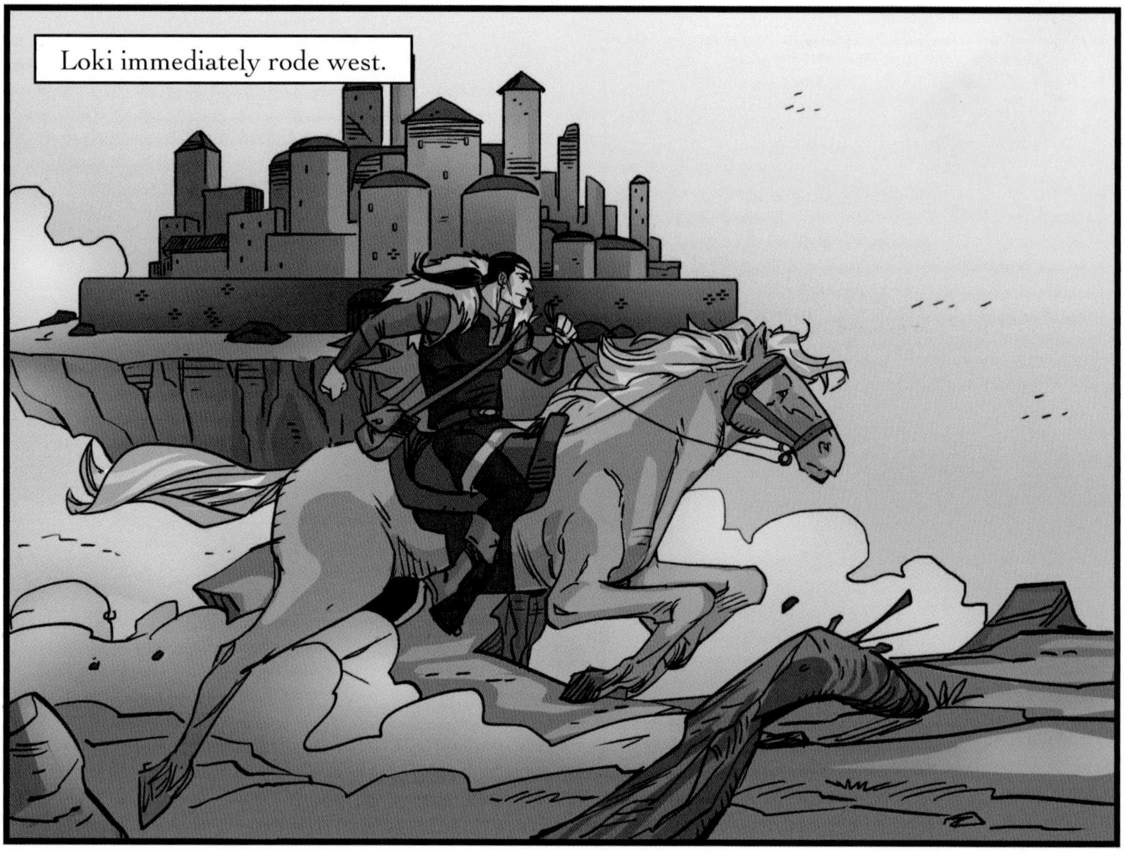
Loki immediately rode west.

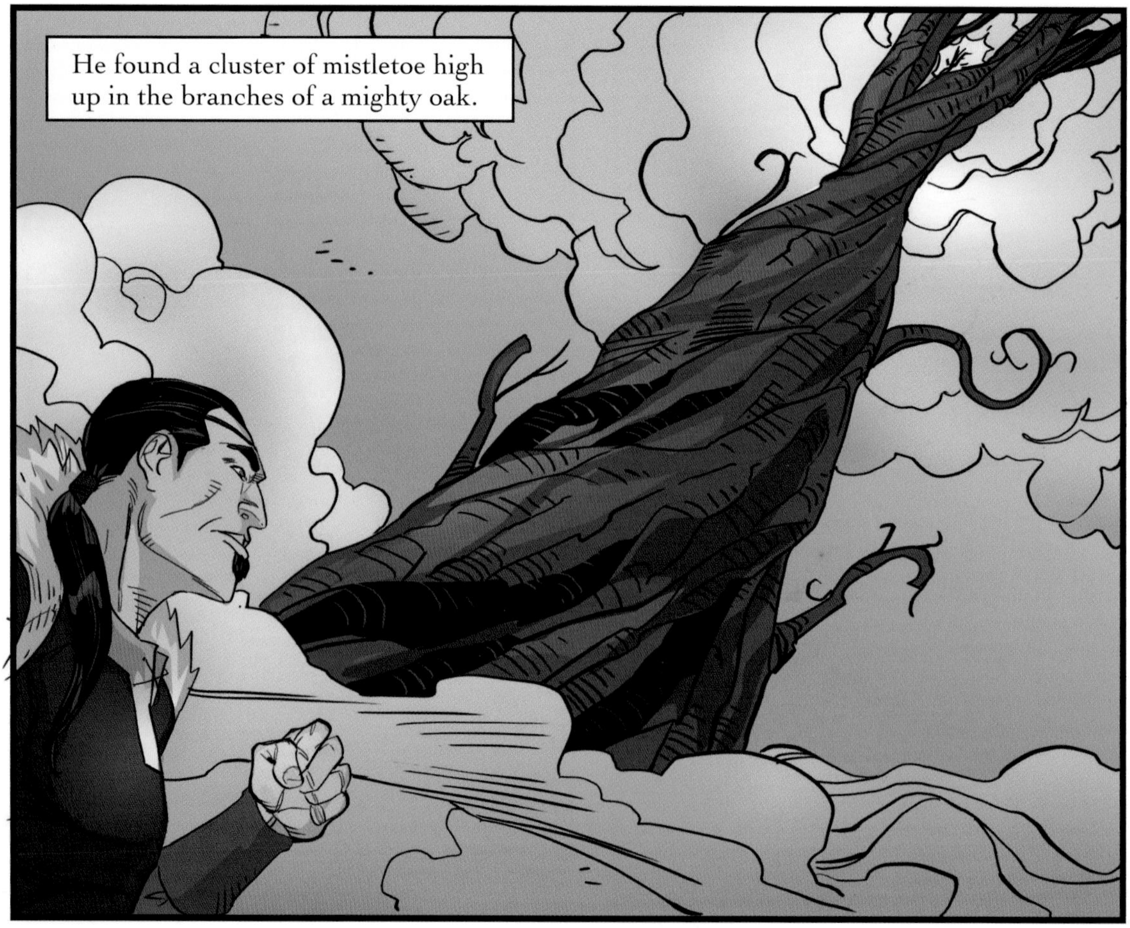
He found a cluster of mistletoe high up in the branches of a mighty oak.

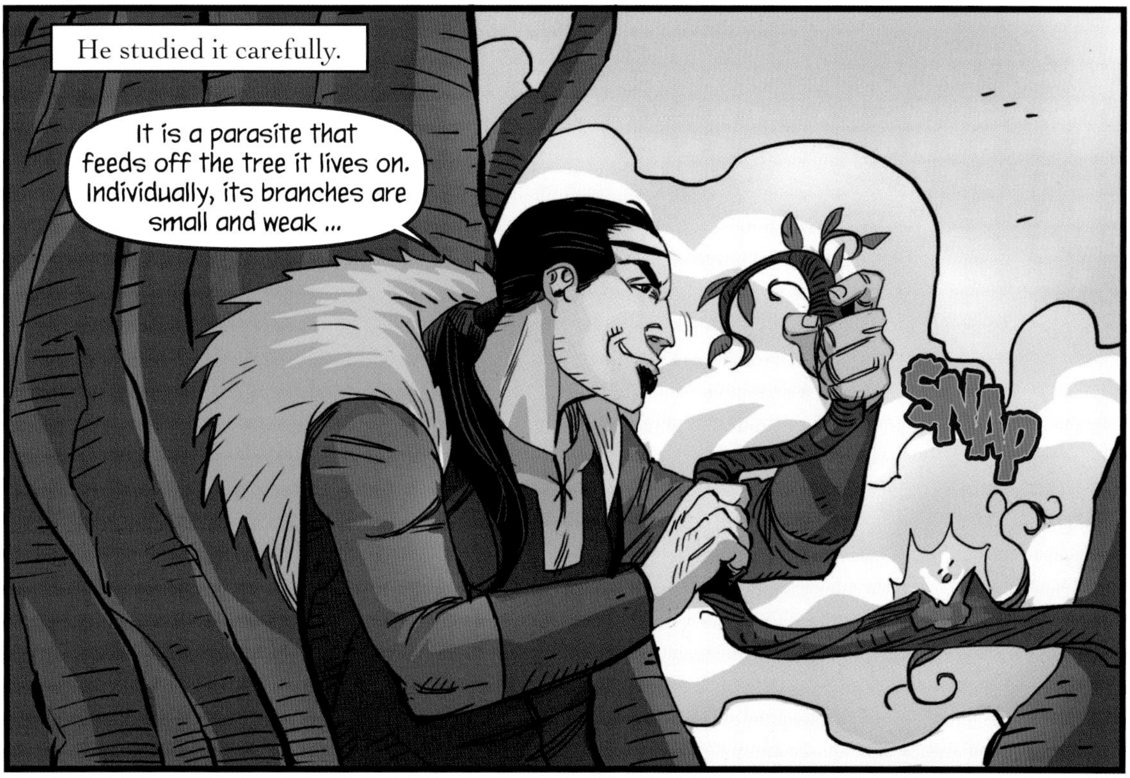
He studied it carefully.
It is a parasite that feeds off the tree it lives on. Individually, its branches are small and weak ...
SNAP

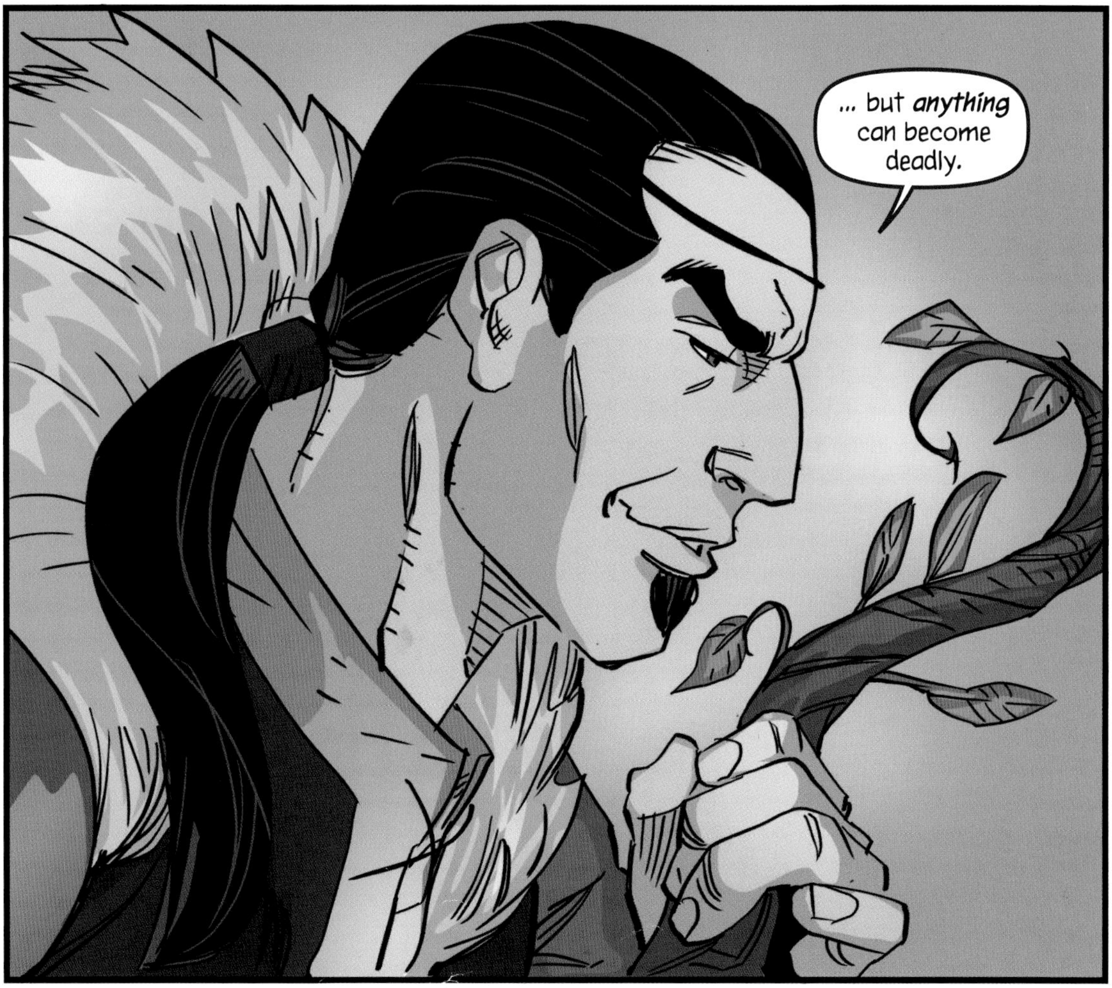
... but *anything* can become deadly.

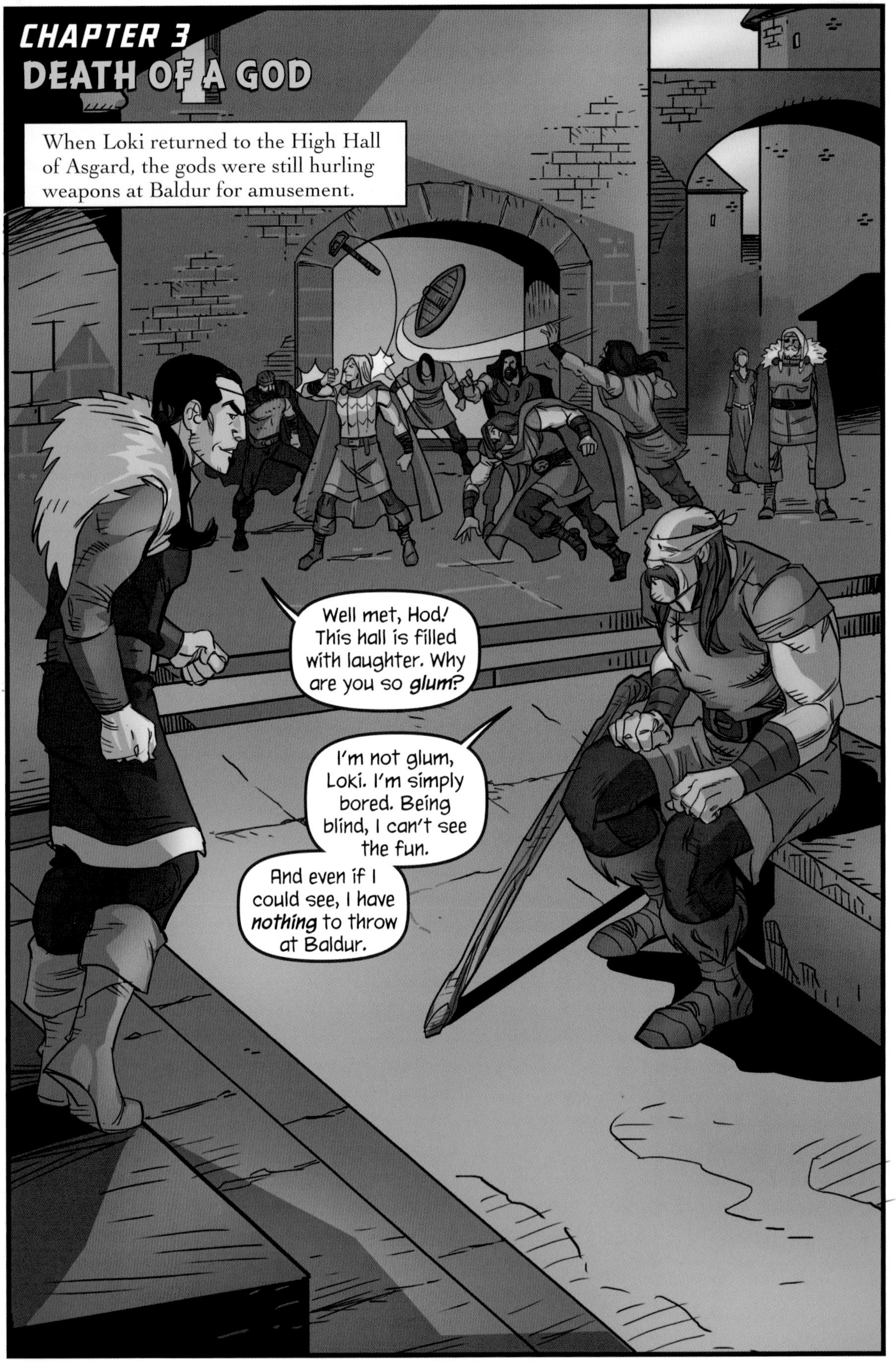
CHAPTER 3
DEATH OF A GOD
When Loki returned to the High Hall of Asgard, the gods were still hurling weapons at Baldur for amusement.
Well met, Hod! This hall is filled with laughter. Why are you so glum?
I'm not glum, Loki. I'm simply bored. Being blind, I can't see the fun.
And even if I could see, I have nothing to throw at Baldur.

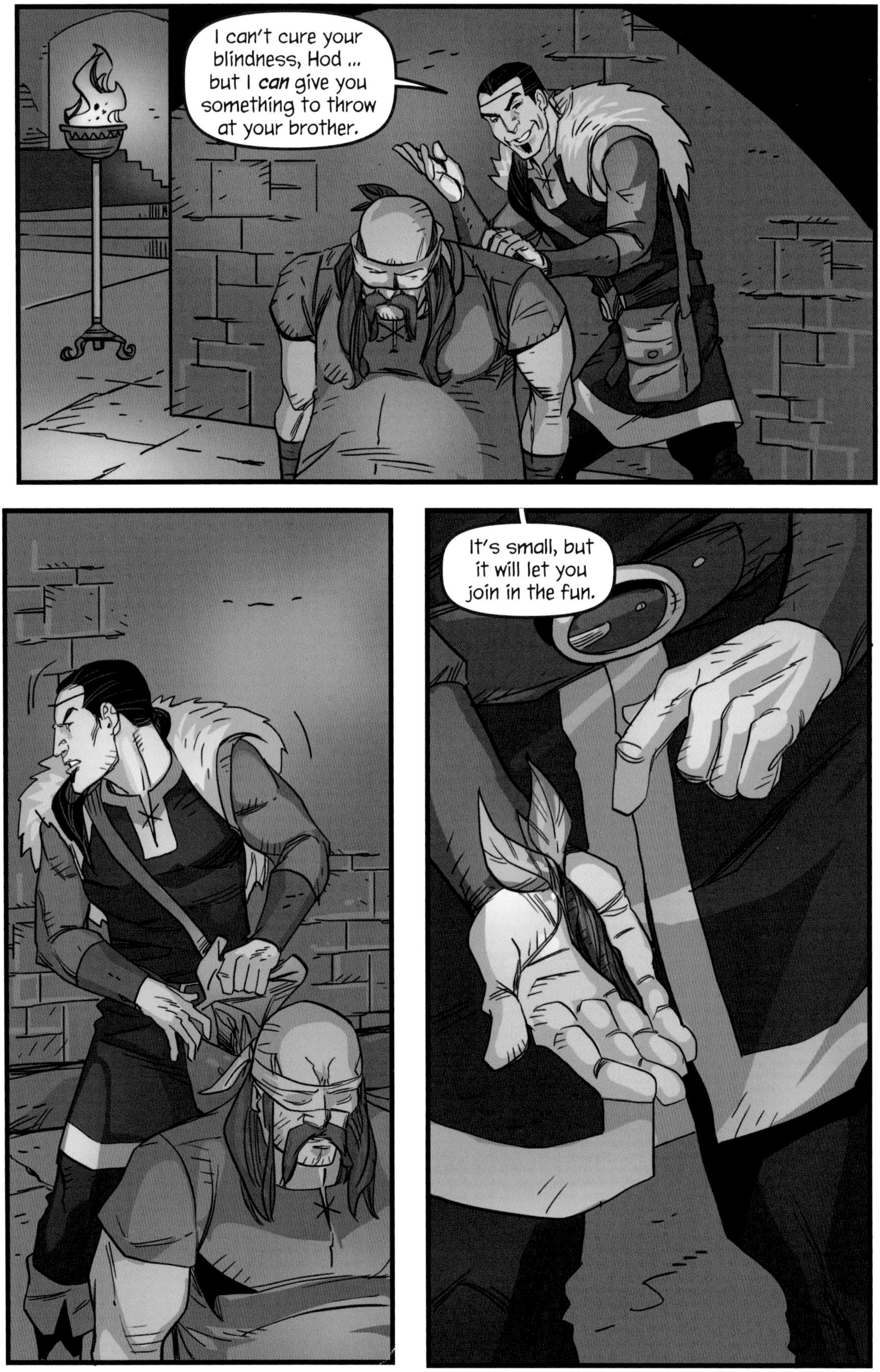
I can't cure your blindness, Hod ... but I *can* give you something to throw at your brother.
It's small, but it will let you join in the fun.

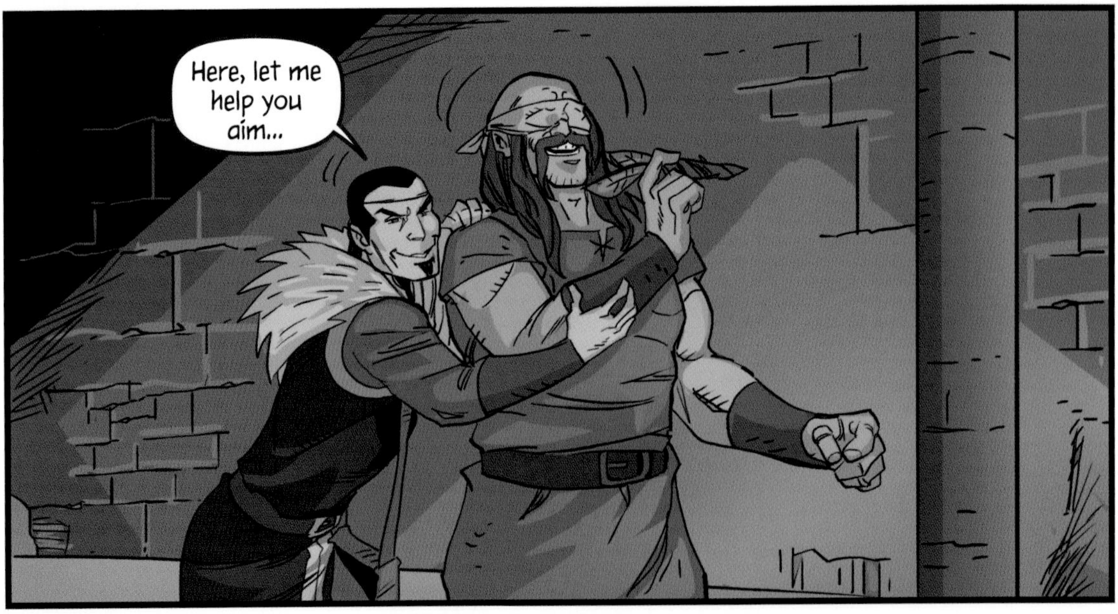
Here, let me help you aim...

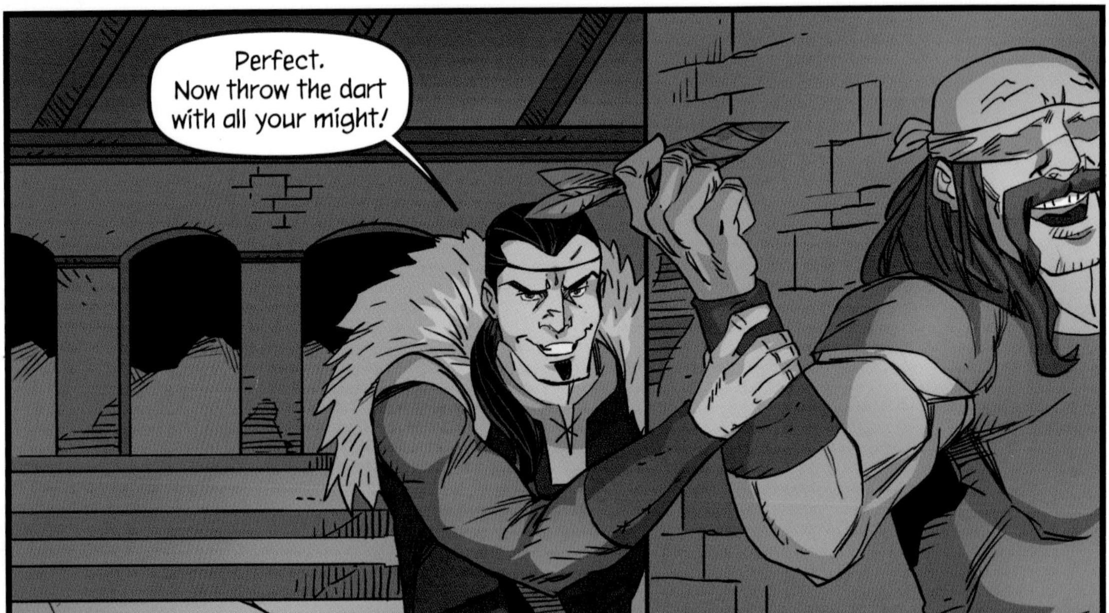
Perfect. Now throw the dart with all your might!

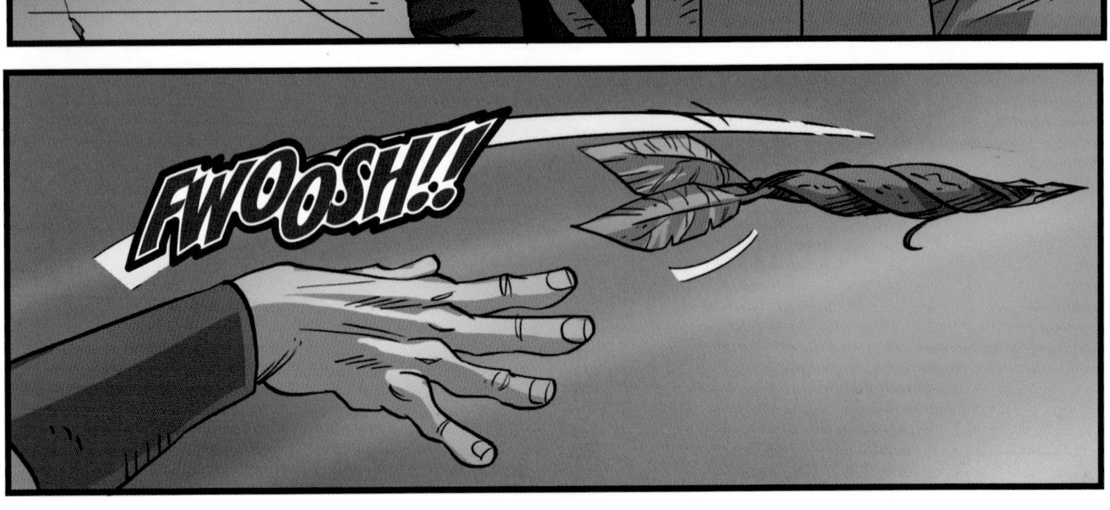
FWOOSH!!

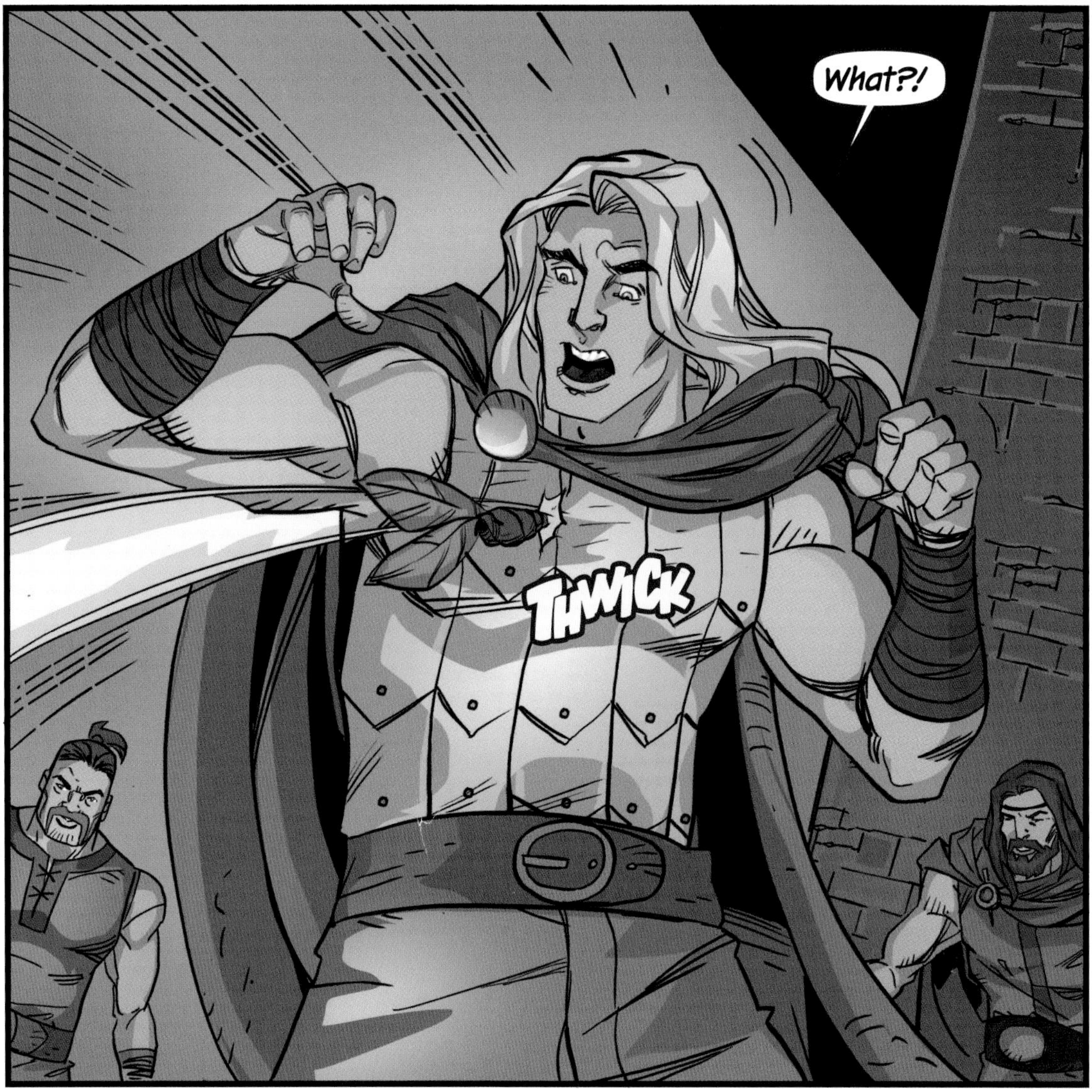
What?!
THWICK

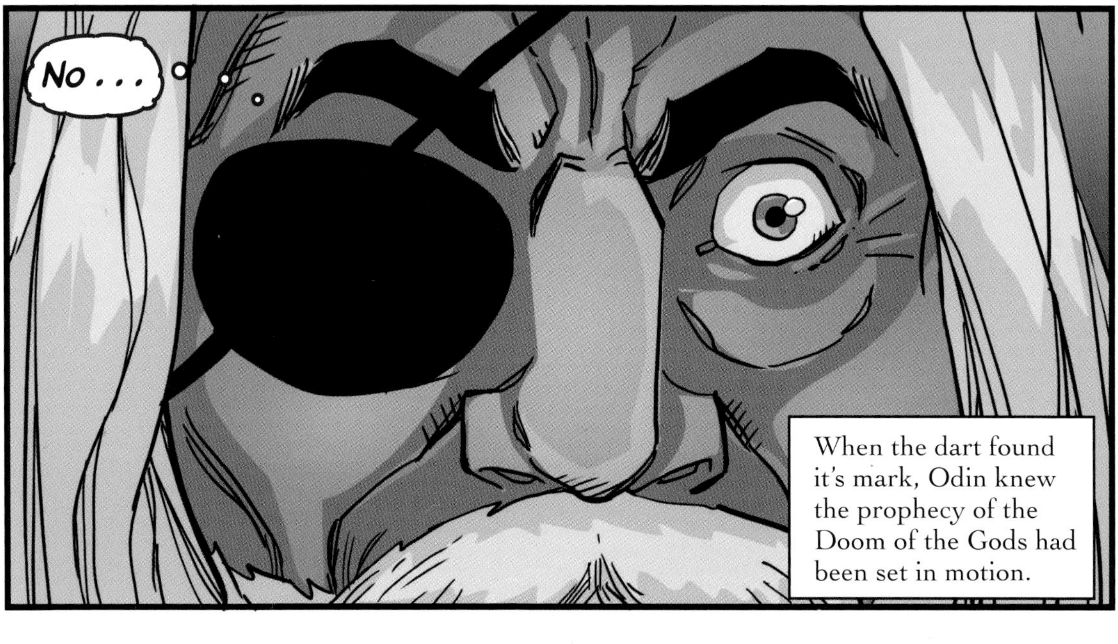
No . . .
When the dart found it's mark, Odin knew the prophecy of the Doom of the Gods had been set in motion.

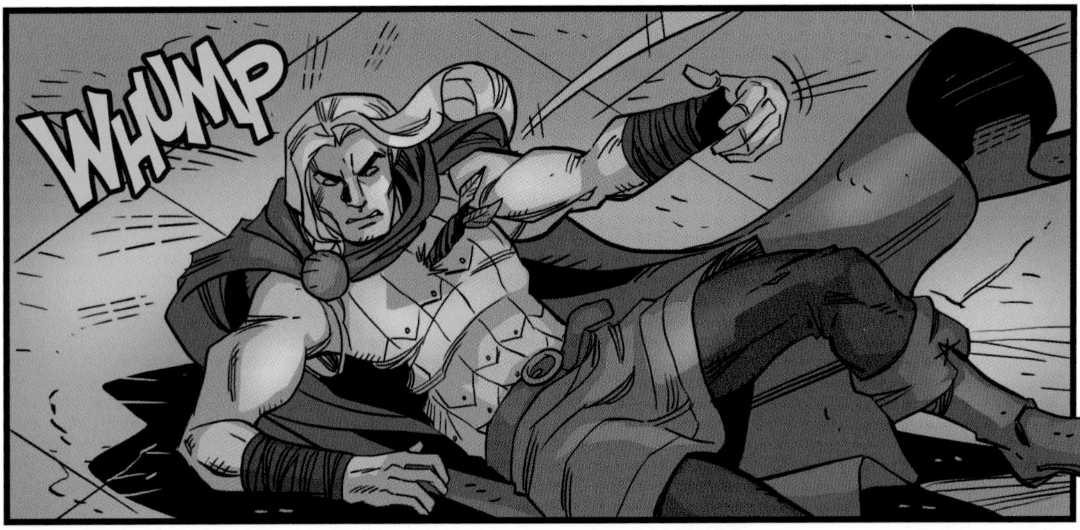
WHUMP

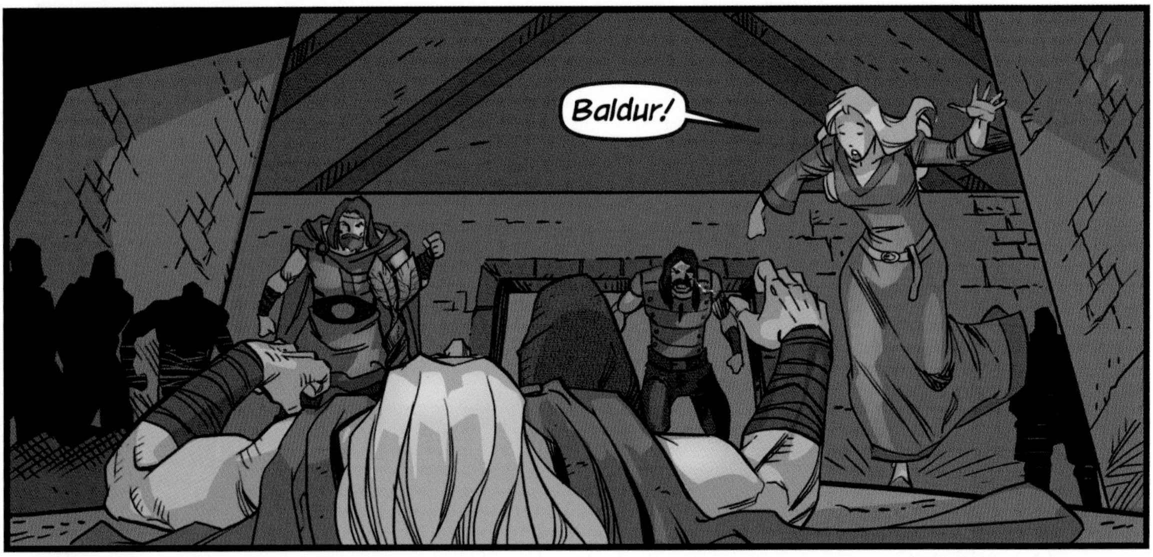
Baldur!

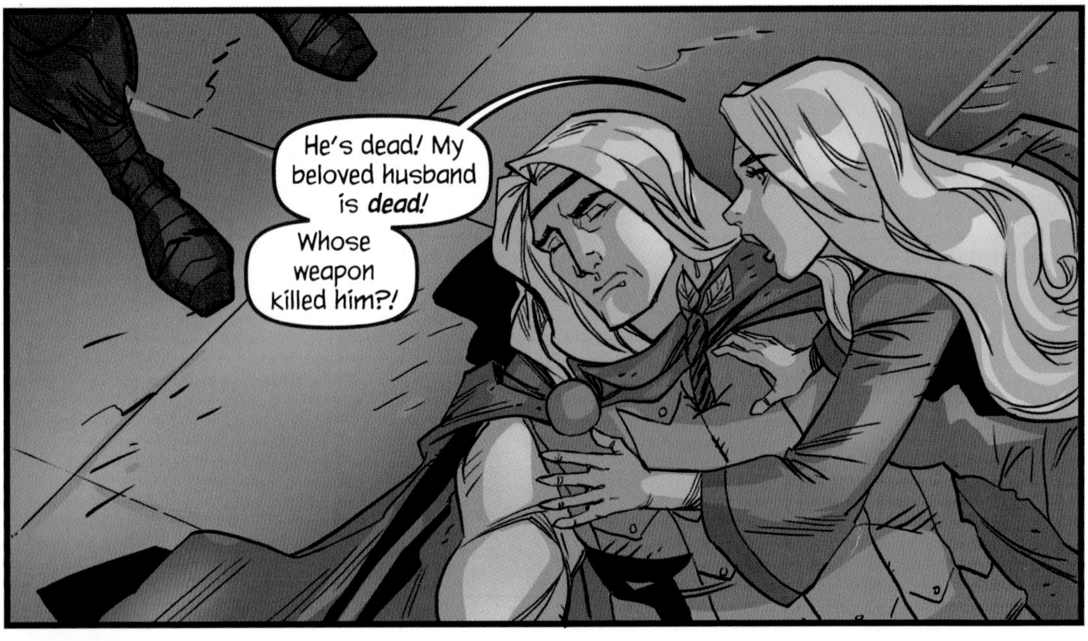
He's dead! My beloved husband is *dead!*
Whose weapon killed him?!

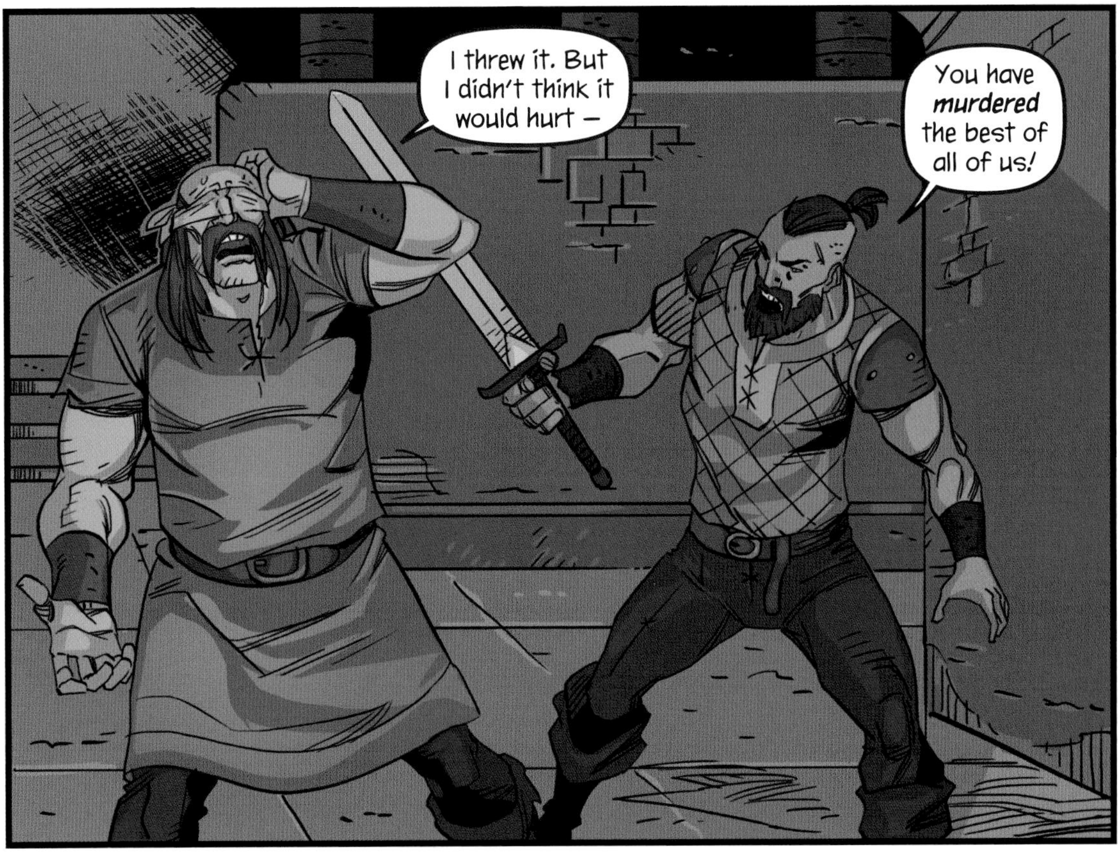
I threw it. But I didn't think it would hurt —
You have **murdered** the best of all of us!

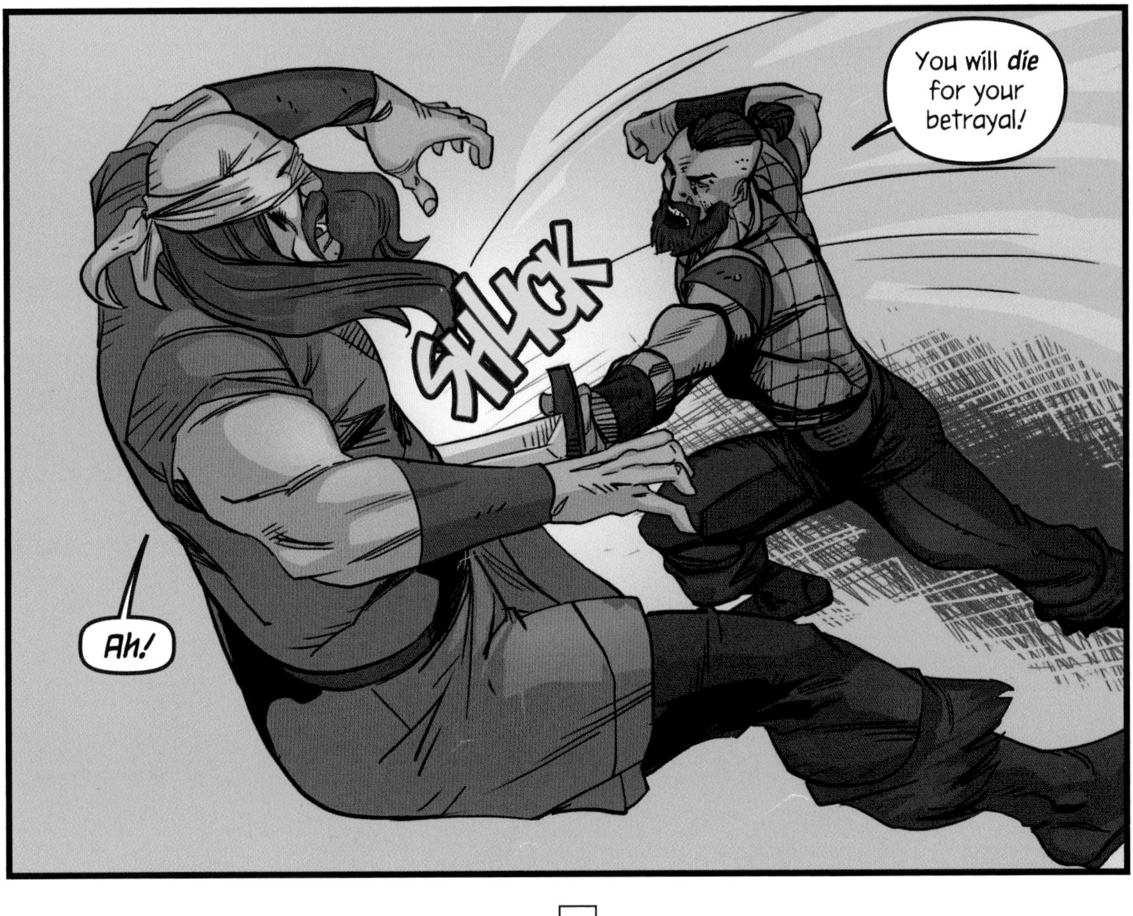
You will **die** for your betrayal!
SHLUCK
Ah!

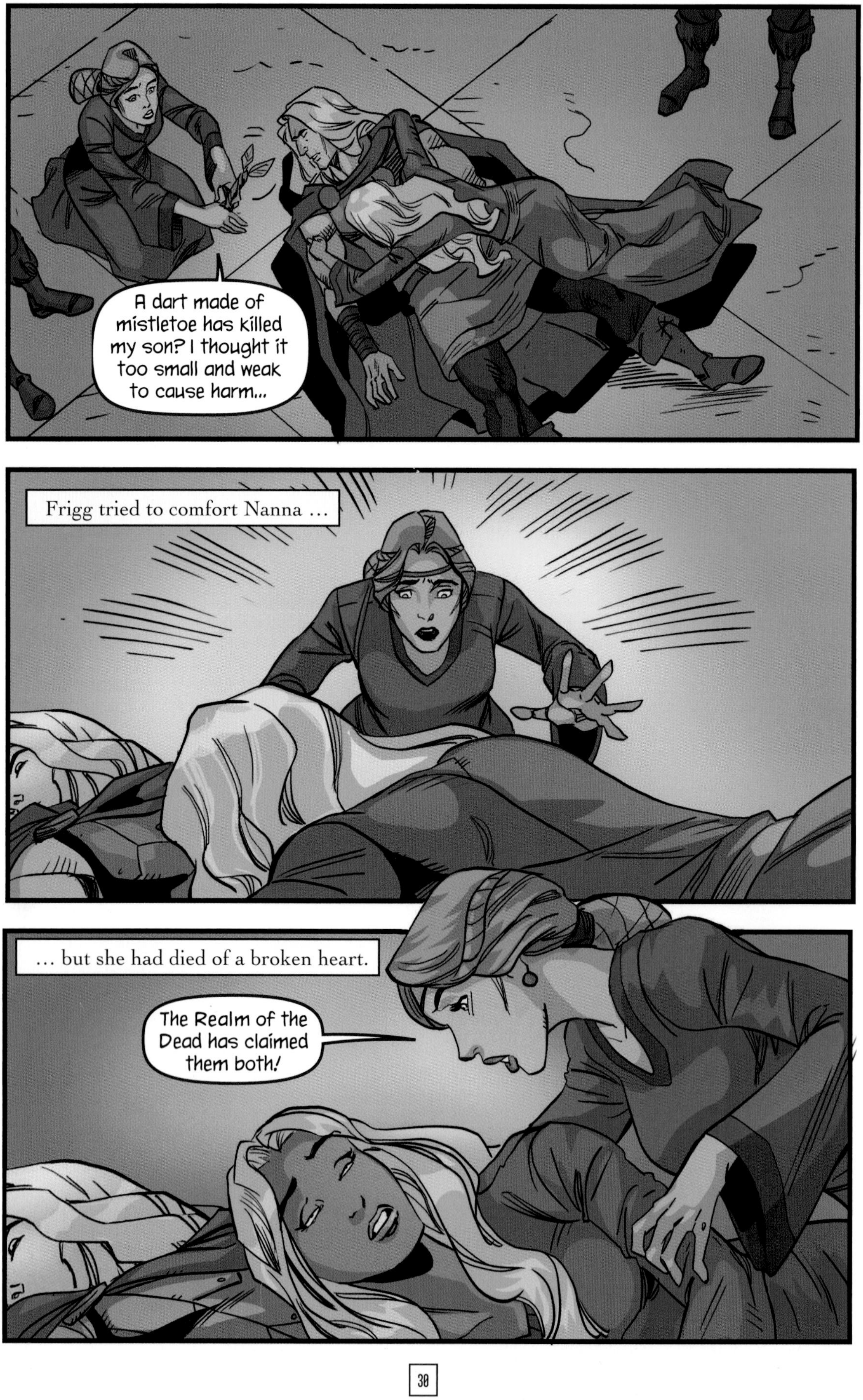
A dart made of mistletoe has killed my son? I thought it too small and weak to cause harm...
Frigg tried to comfort Nanna …
… but she had died of a broken heart.
The Realm of the Dead has claimed them both!

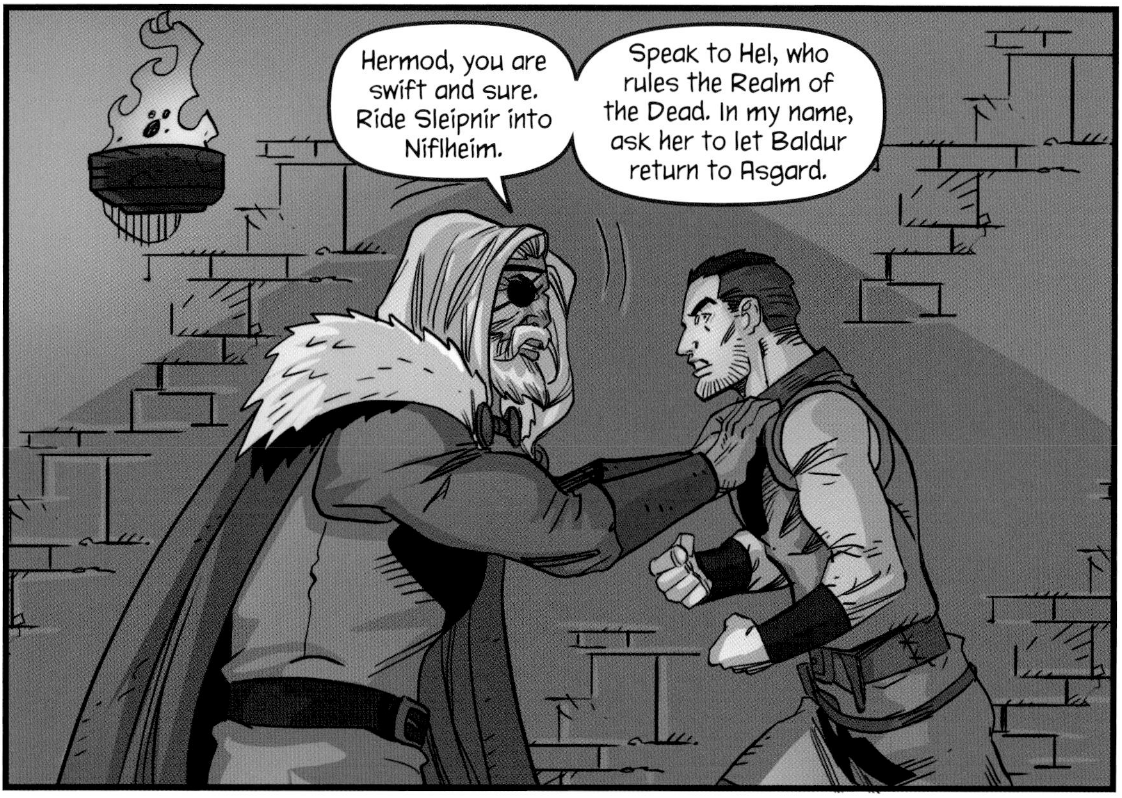
Hermod, you are swift and sure. Ride Sleipnir into Niflheim.
Speak to Hel, who rules the Realm of the Dead. In my name, ask her to let Baldur return to Asgard.

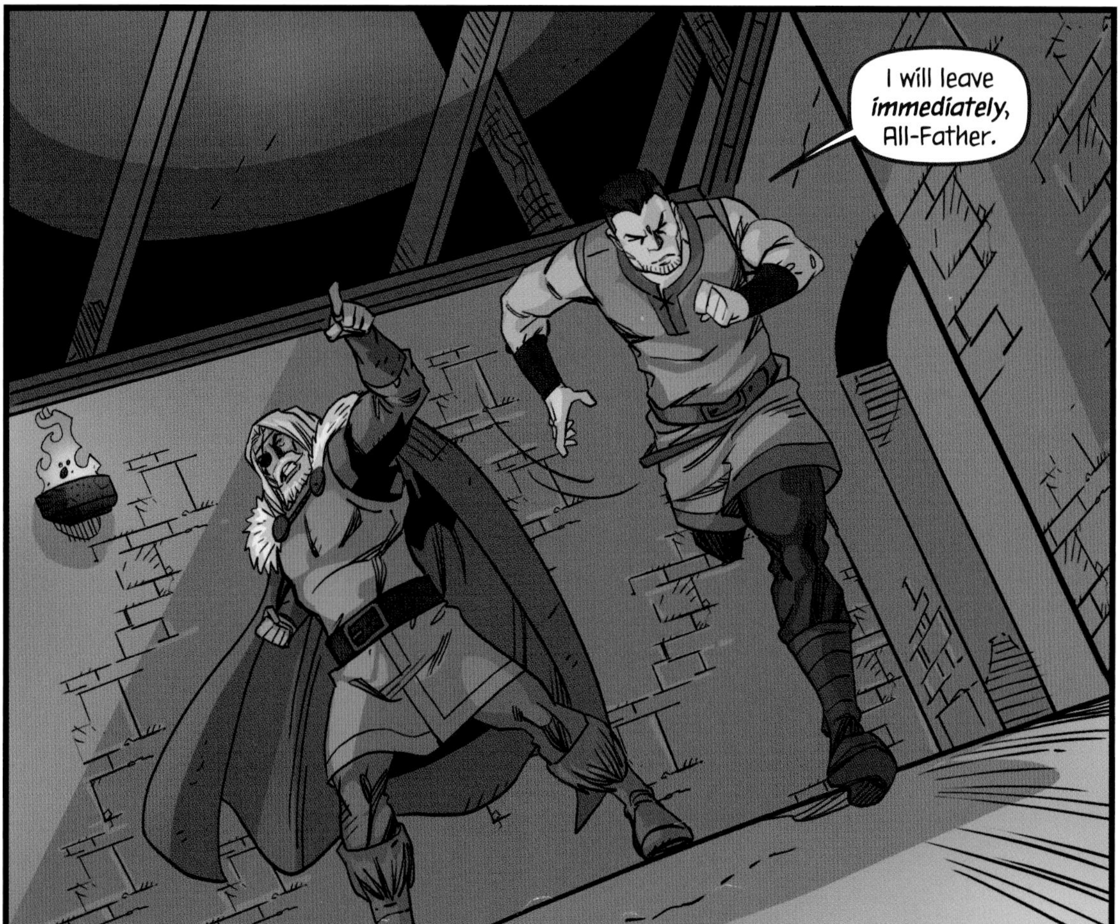
I will leave *immediately*, All-Father.

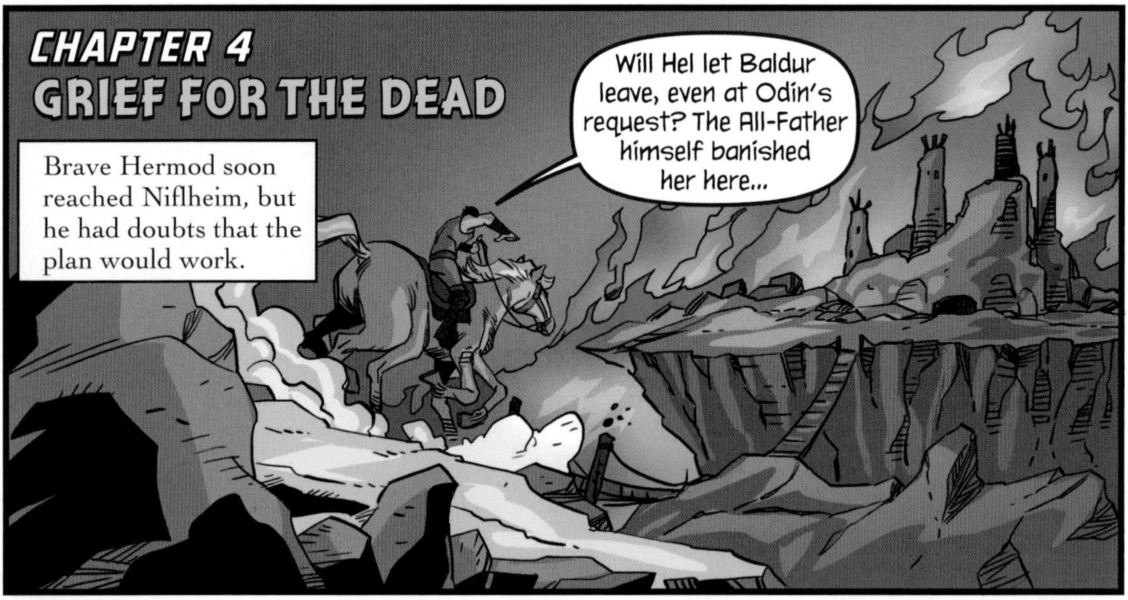
CHAPTER 4
GRIEF FOR THE DEAD
Brave Hermod soon reached Niflheim, but he had doubts that the plan would work.
Will Hel let Baldur leave, even at Odin's request? The All-Father himself banished her here...

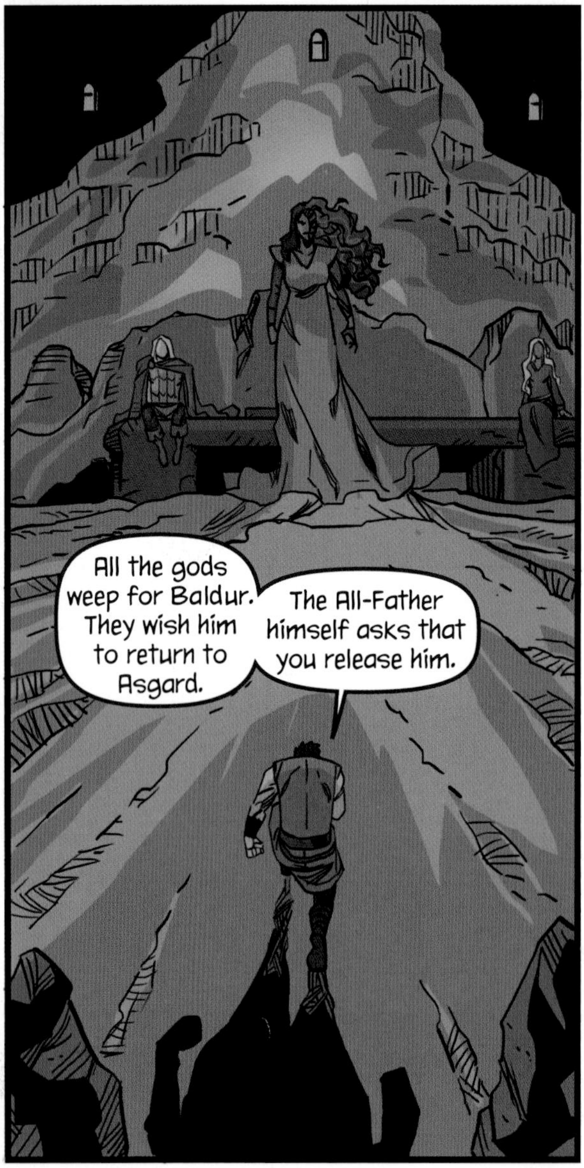
All the gods weep for Baldur. They wish him to return to Asgard.
The All-Father himself asks that you release him.

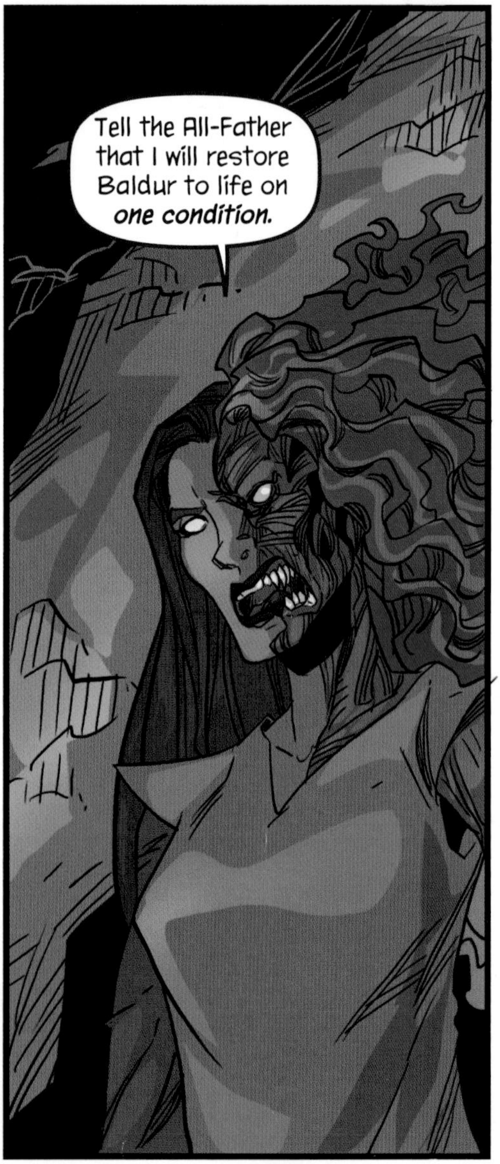
Tell the All-Father that I will restore Baldur to life on *one condition.*

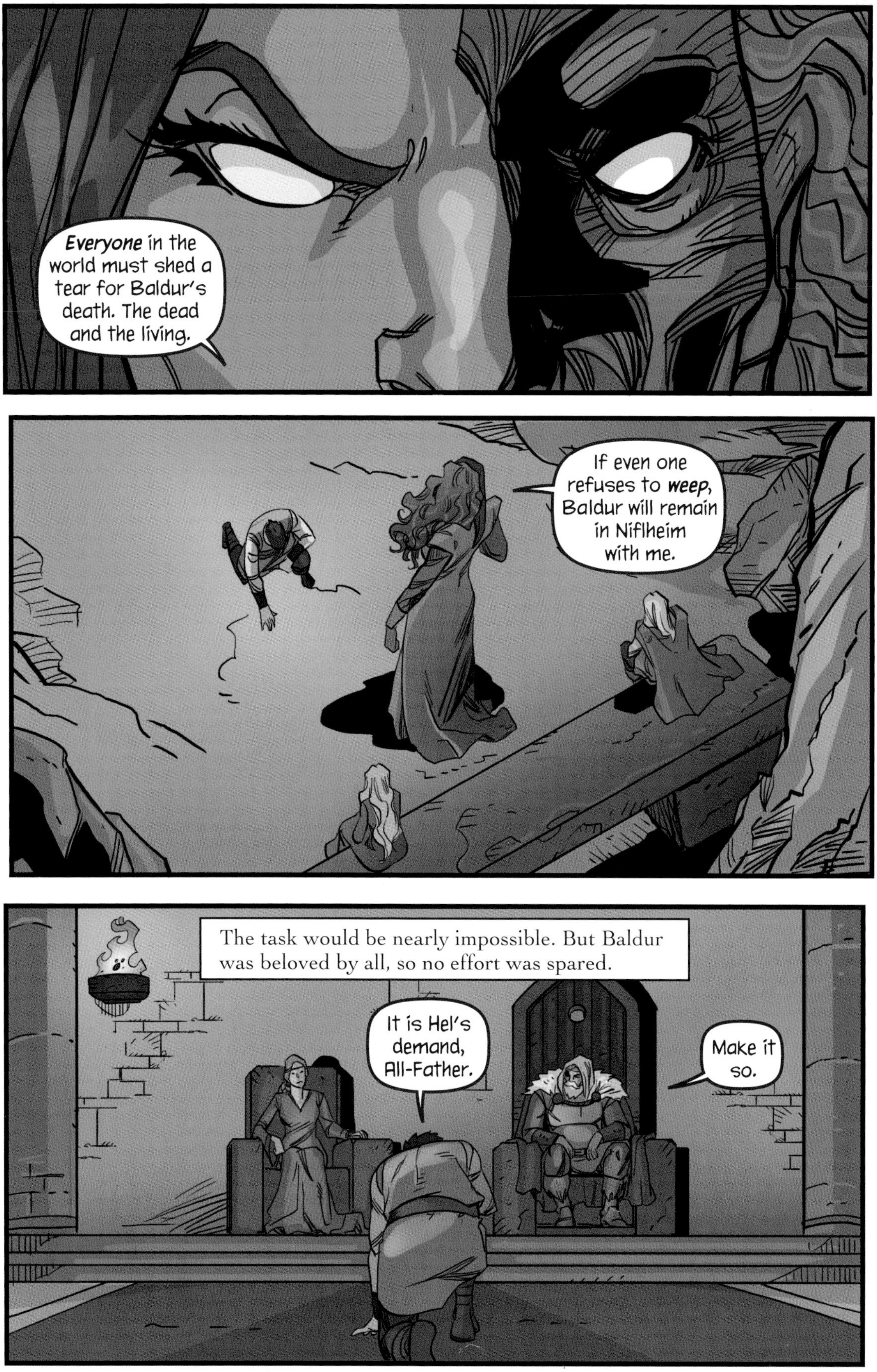

Everyone in the world must shed a tear for Baldur's death. The dead and the living.
If even one refuses to *weep*, Baldur will remain in Niflheim with me.
The task would be nearly impossible. But Baldur was beloved by all, so no effort was spared.
It is Hel's demand, All-Father.
Make it so.

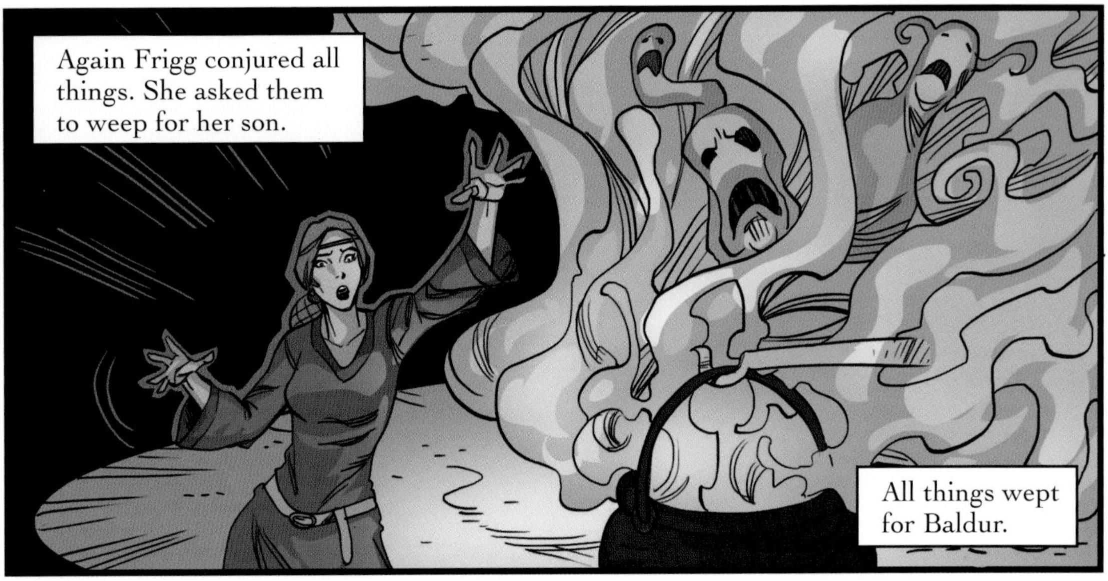
Again Frigg conjured all things. She asked them to weep for her son.
All things wept for Baldur.

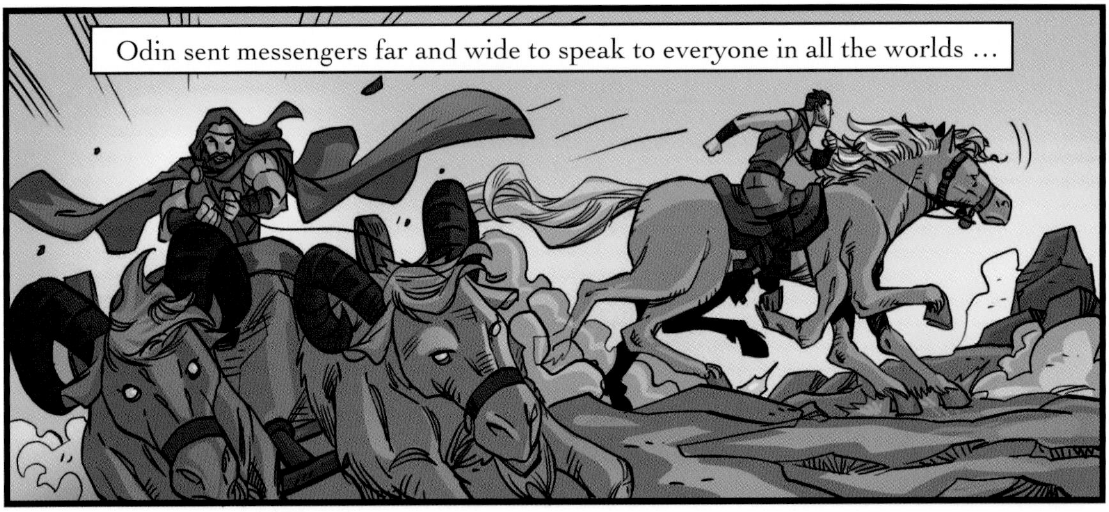
Odin sent messengers far and wide to speak to everyone in all the worlds …

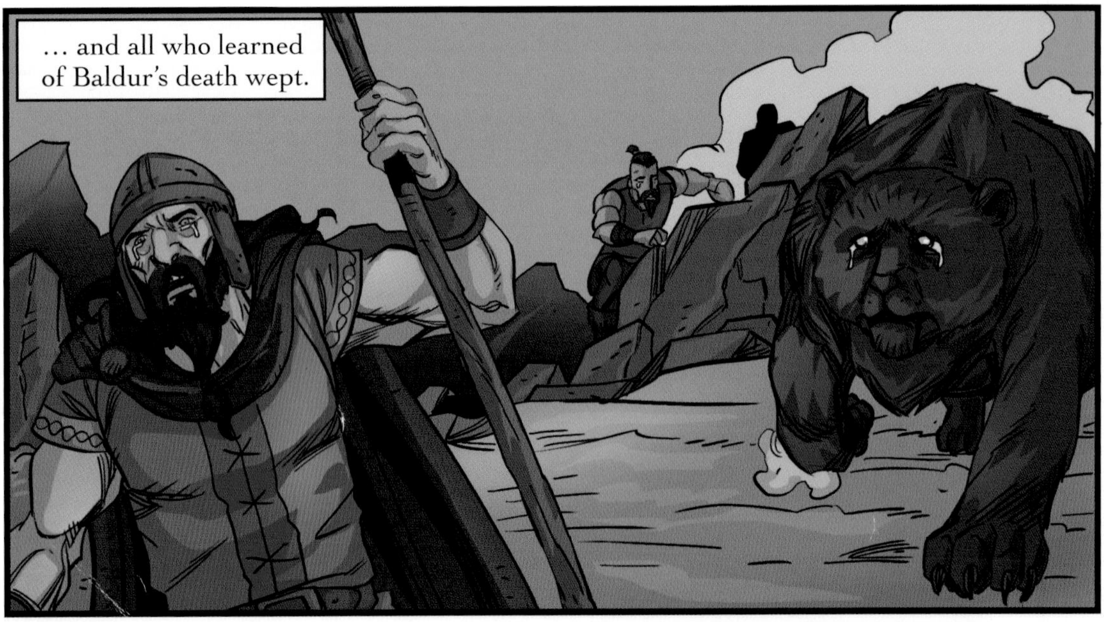
… and all who learned of Baldur's death wept.

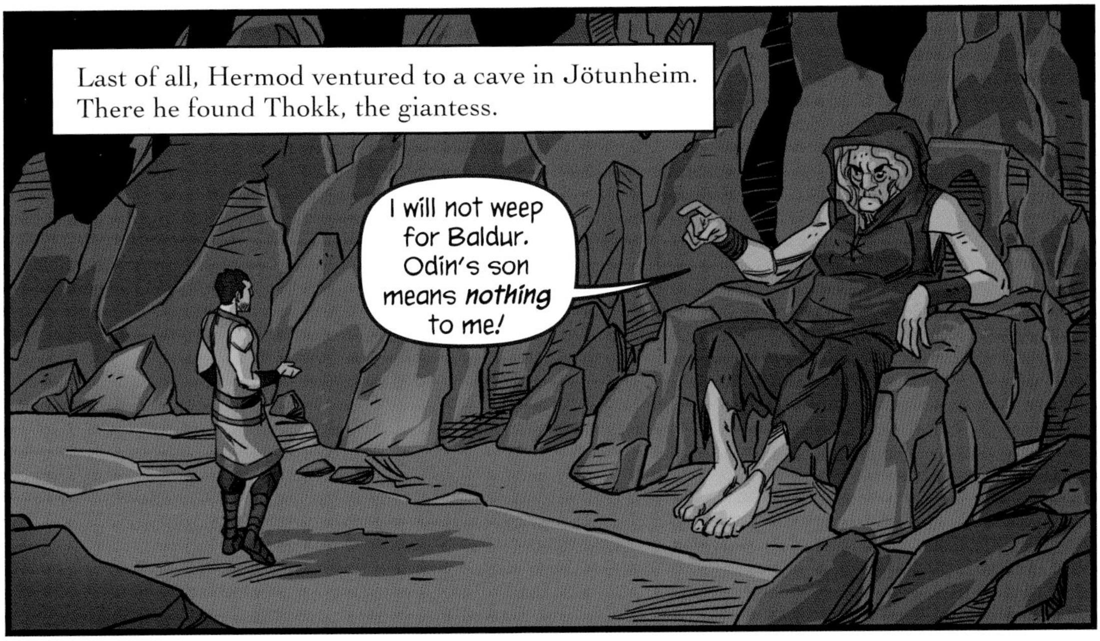
Last of all, Hermod ventured to a cave in Jötunheim. There he found Thokk, the giantess.
I will not weep for Baldur. Odin's son means *nothing* to me!

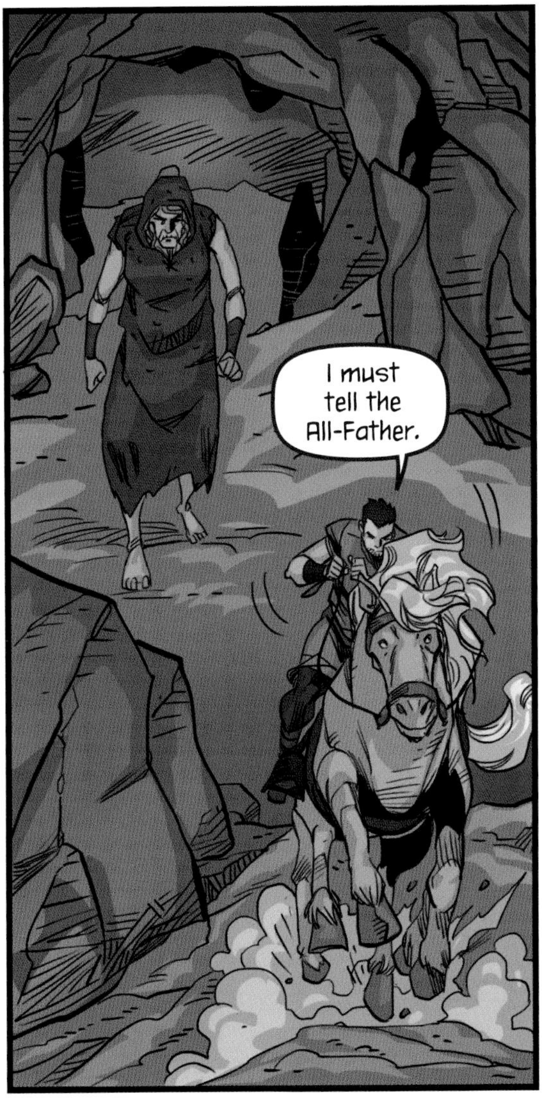
I must tell the All-Father.

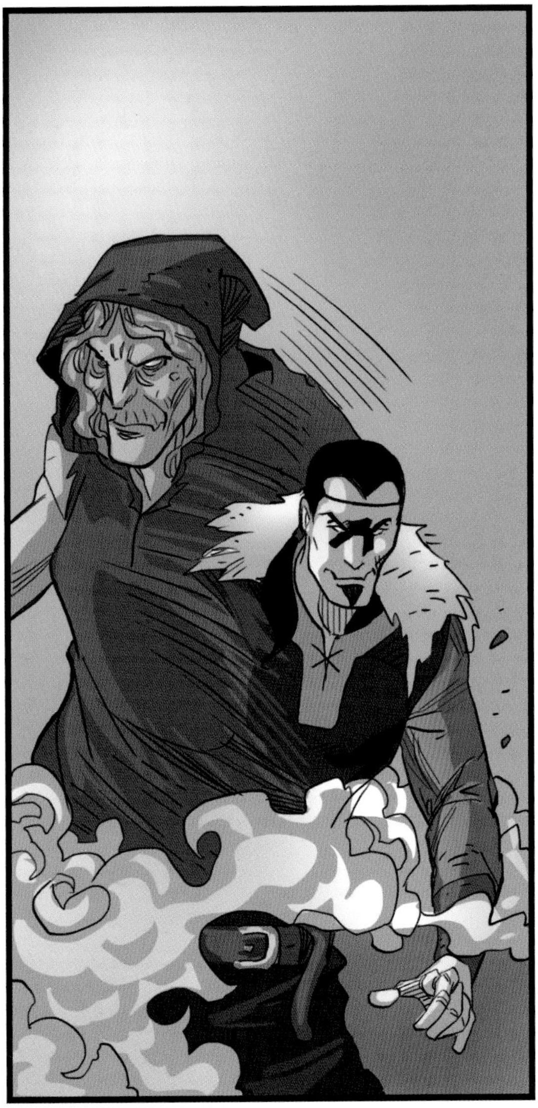

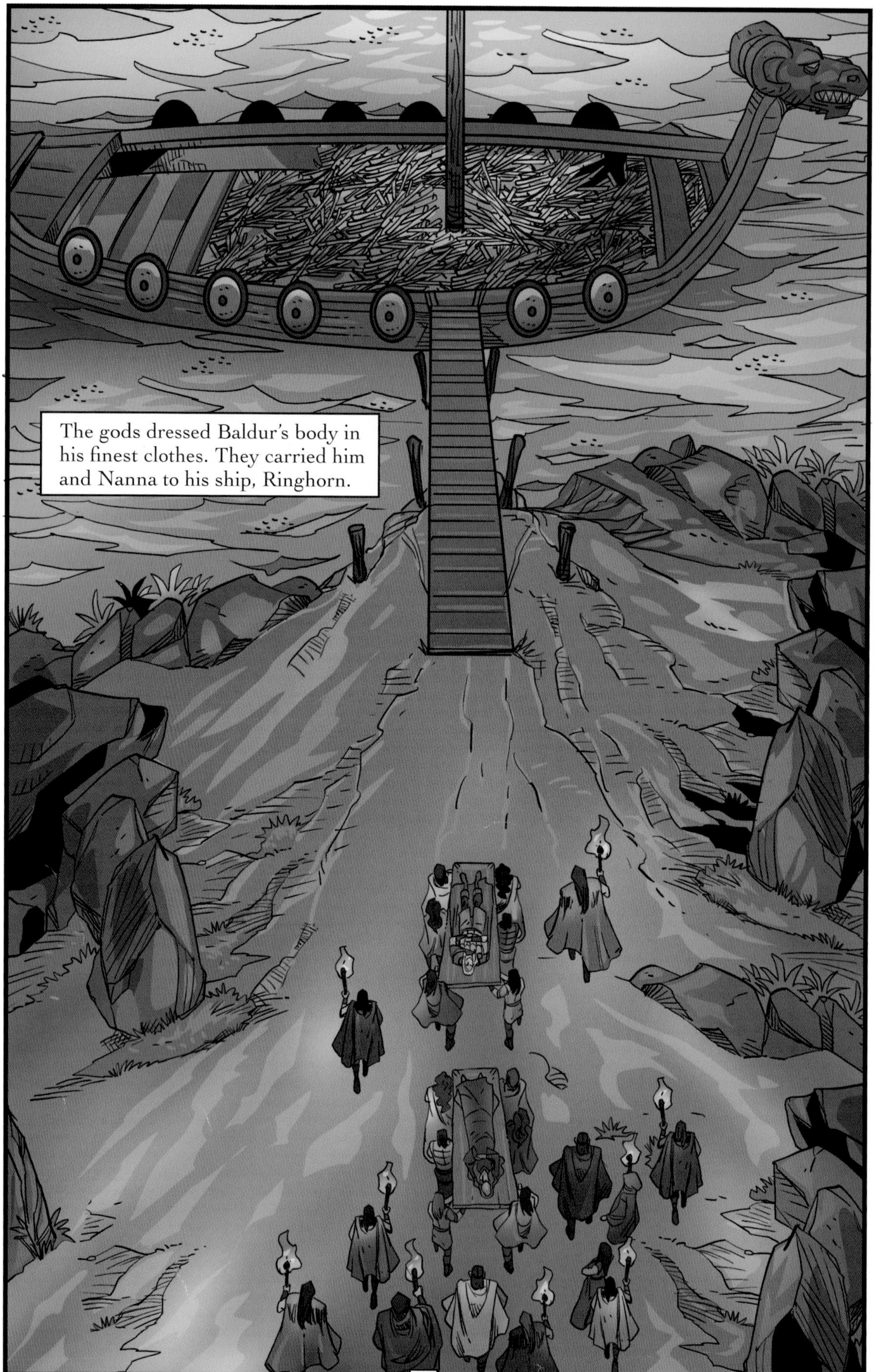
The gods dressed Baldur's body in his finest clothes. They carried him and Nanna to his ship, Ringhorn.

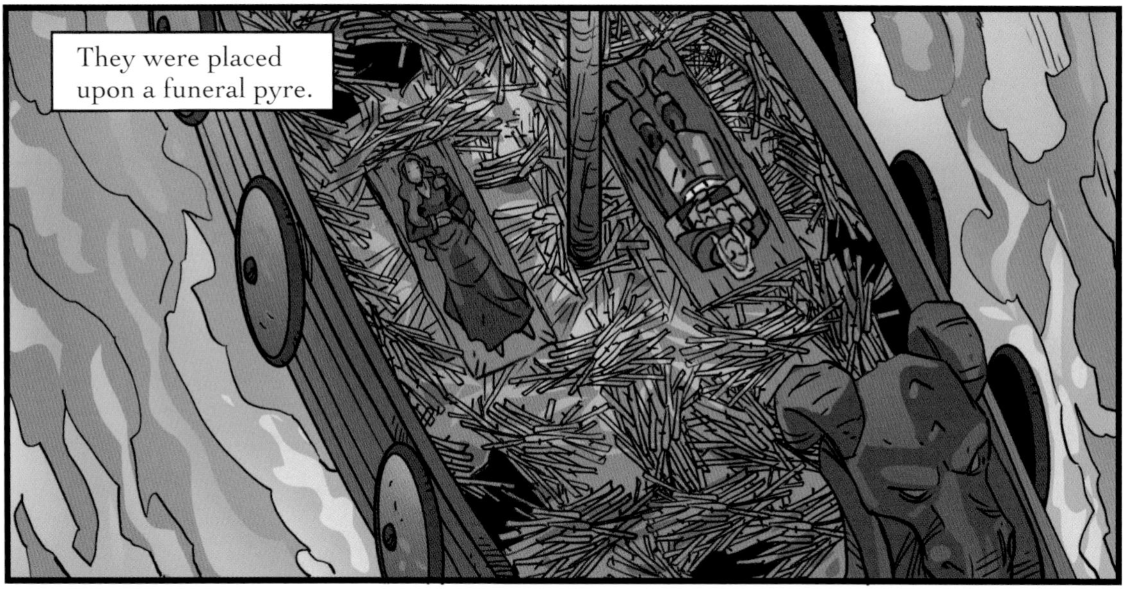
They were placed upon a funeral pyre.

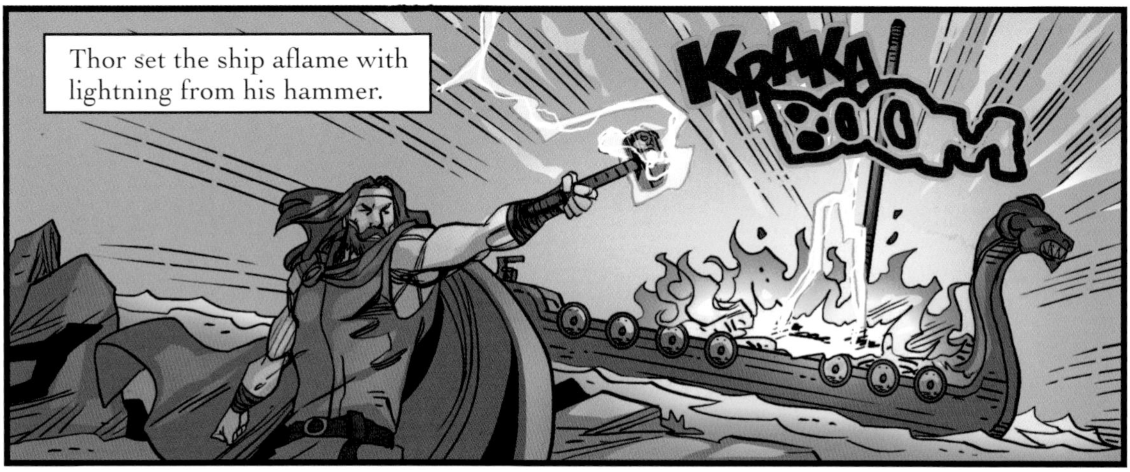
Thor set the ship aflame with lightning from his hammer.
KRAKA BOOM

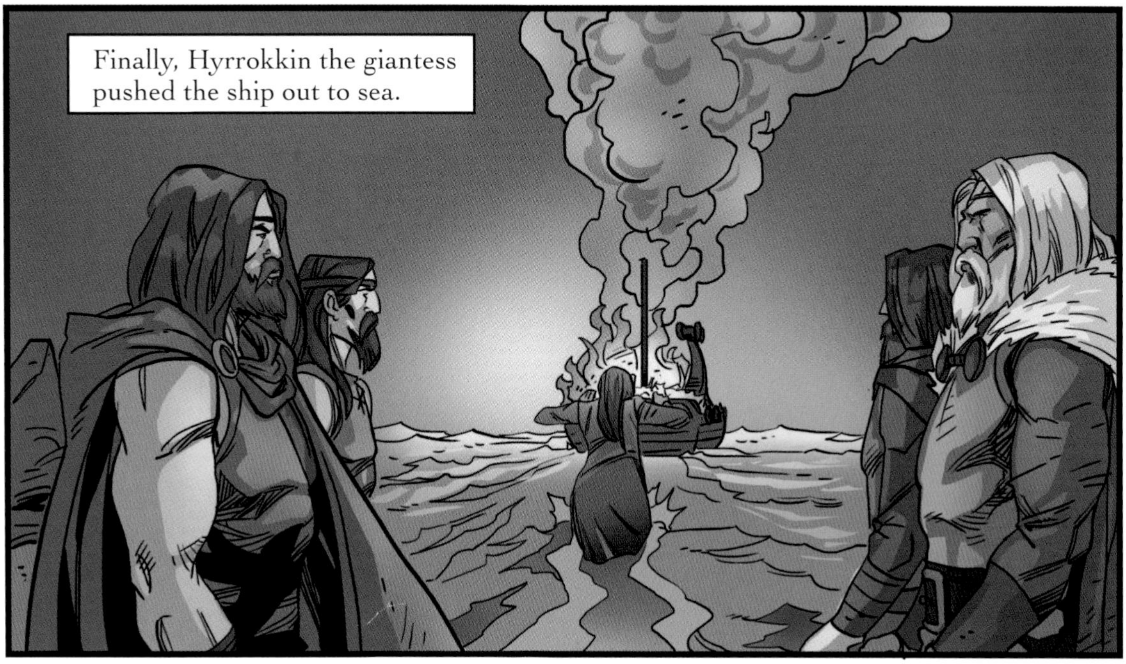
Finally, Hyrrokkin the giantess pushed the ship out to sea.

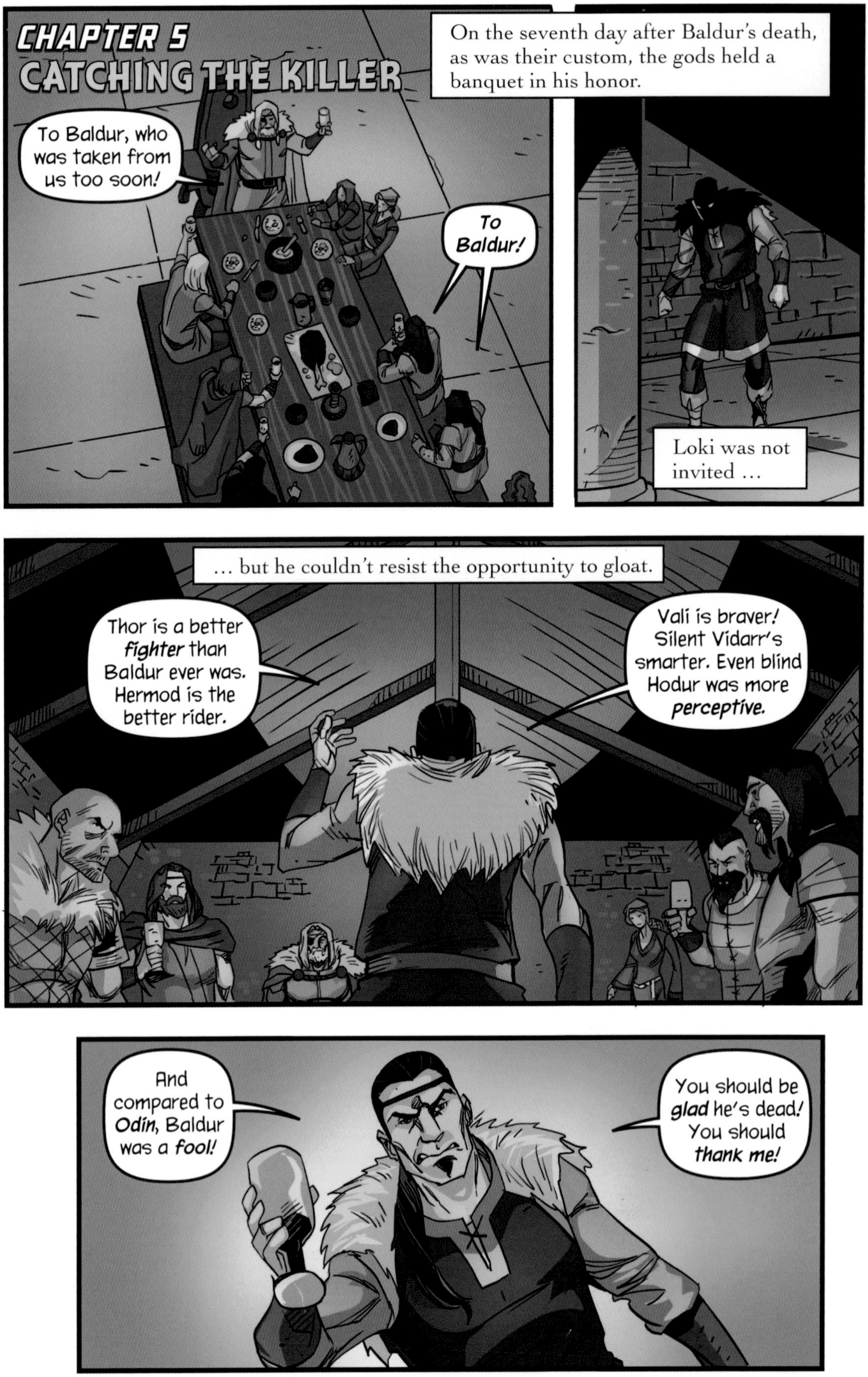
CHAPTER 5
CATCHING THE KILLER
On the seventh day after Baldur's death, as was their custom, the gods held a banquet in his honor.
To Baldur, who was taken from us too soon!
To Baldur!
Loki was not invited …
… but he couldn't resist the opportunity to gloat.
Thor is a better fighter than Baldur ever was. Hermod is the better rider.
Vali is braver! Silent Vidarr's smarter. Even blind Hodur was more perceptive.
And compared to Odin, Baldur was a fool!
You should be glad he's dead! You should thank me!

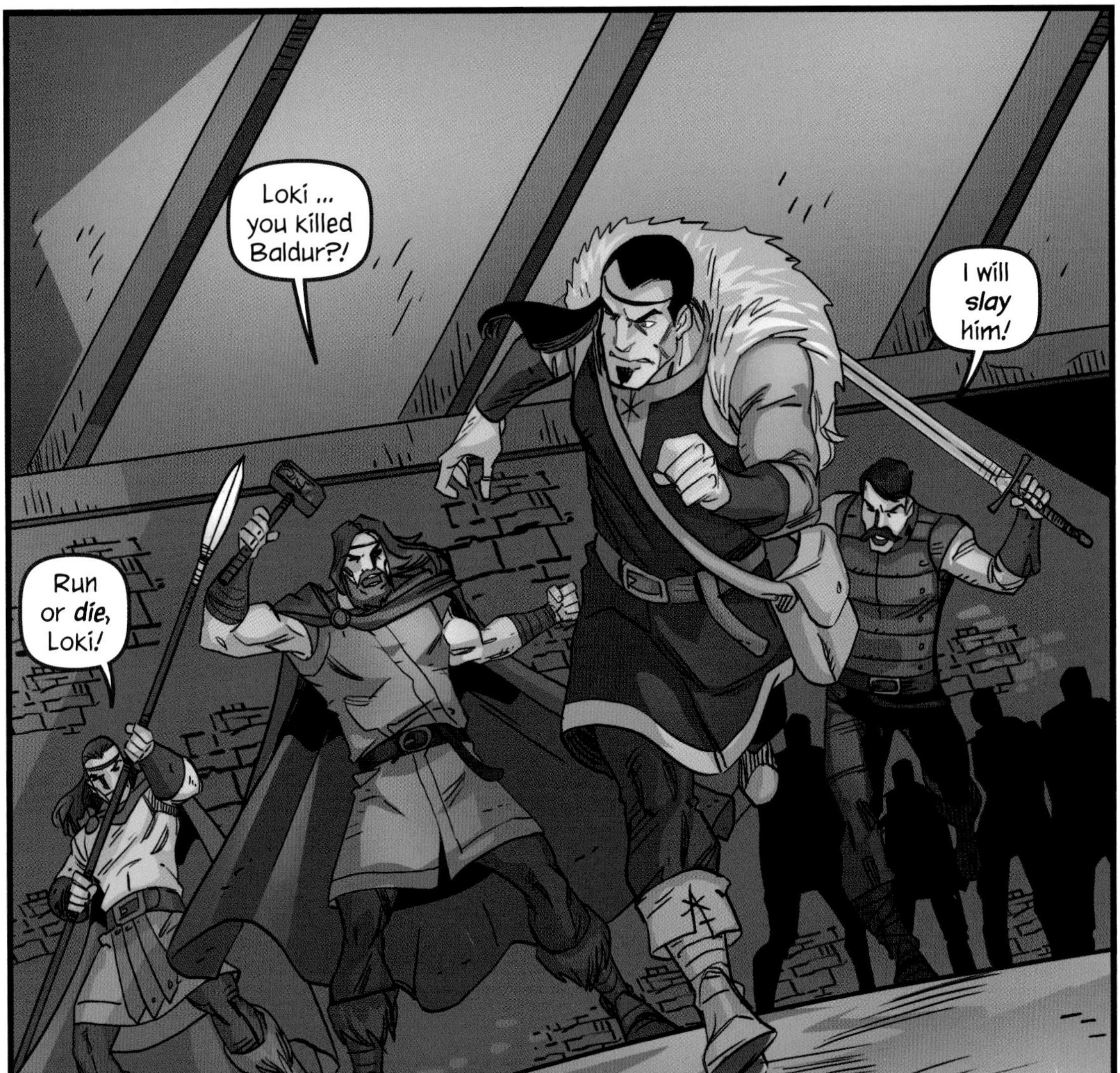
Loki ...
you killed
Baldur?!
I will
slay
him!
Run
or die,
Loki!

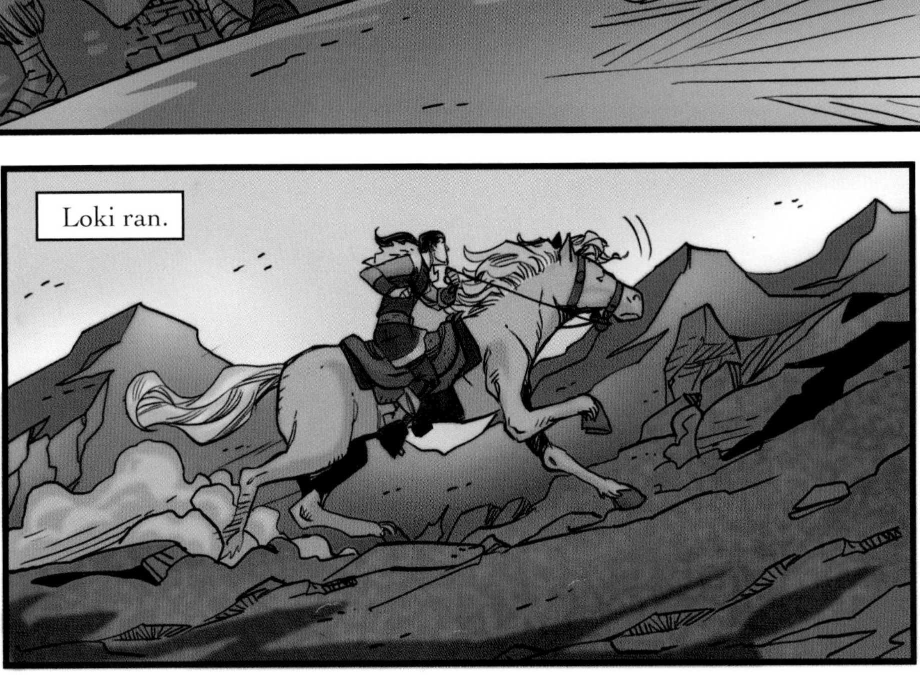
Loki ran.

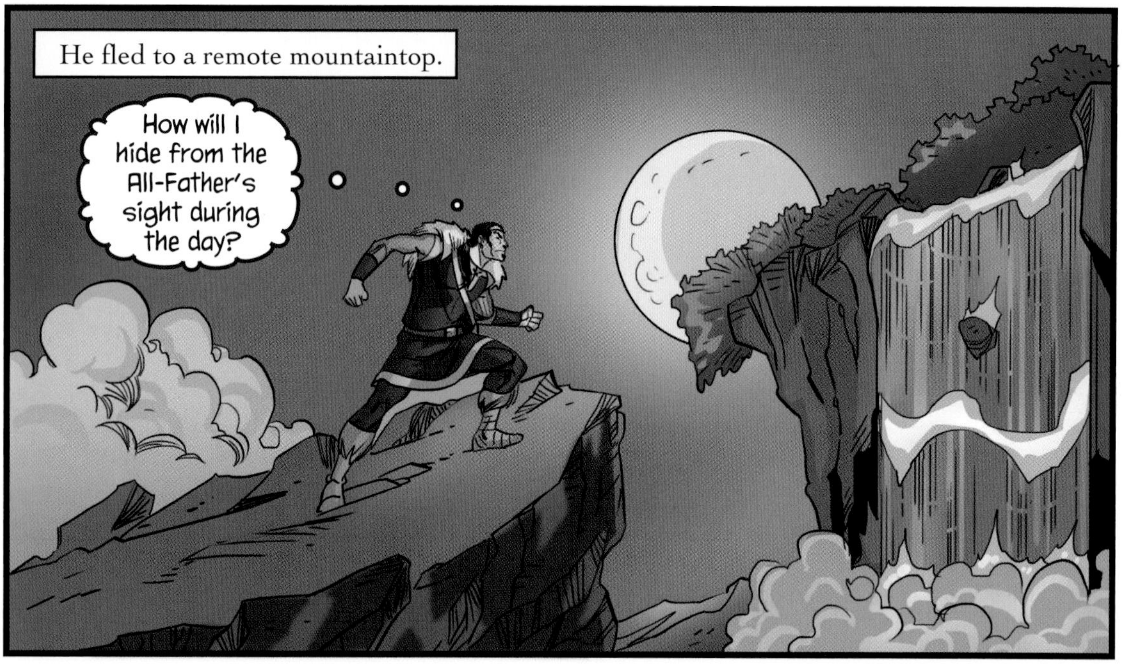
He fled to a remote mountaintop.
How will I hide from the All-Father's sight during the day?

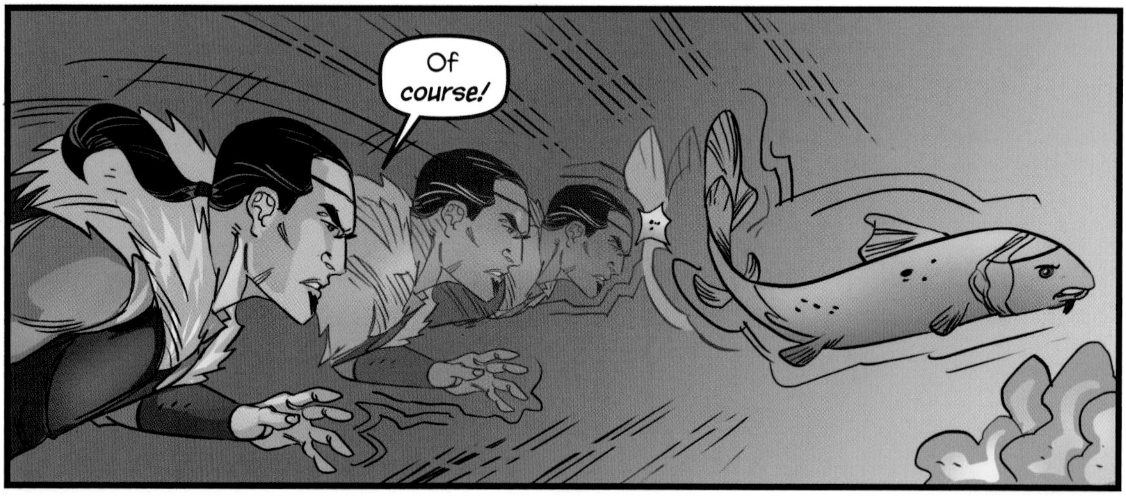
Of *course!*

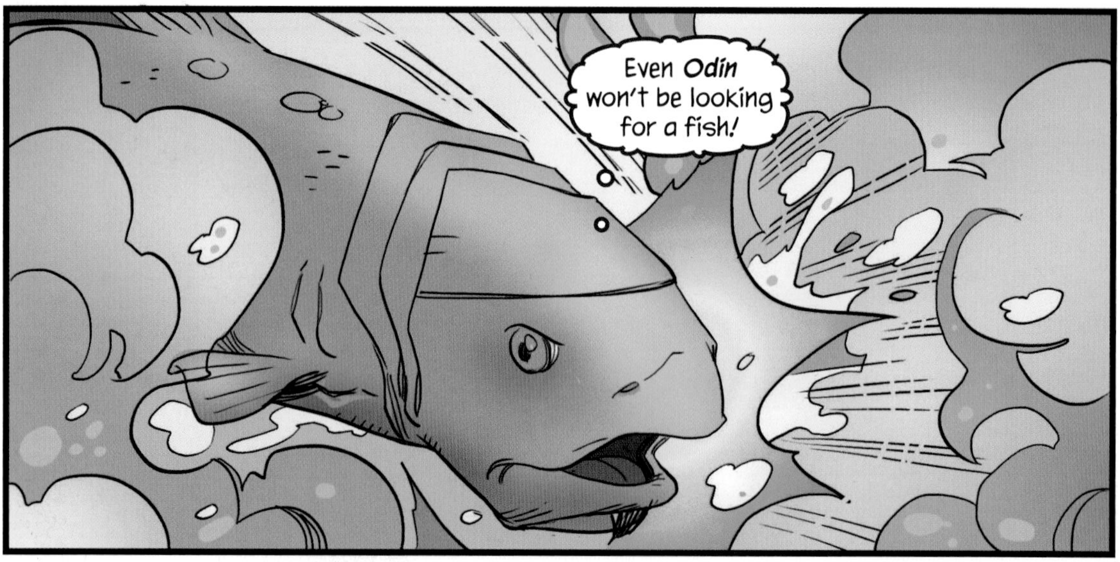
Even *Odin* won't be looking for a fish!

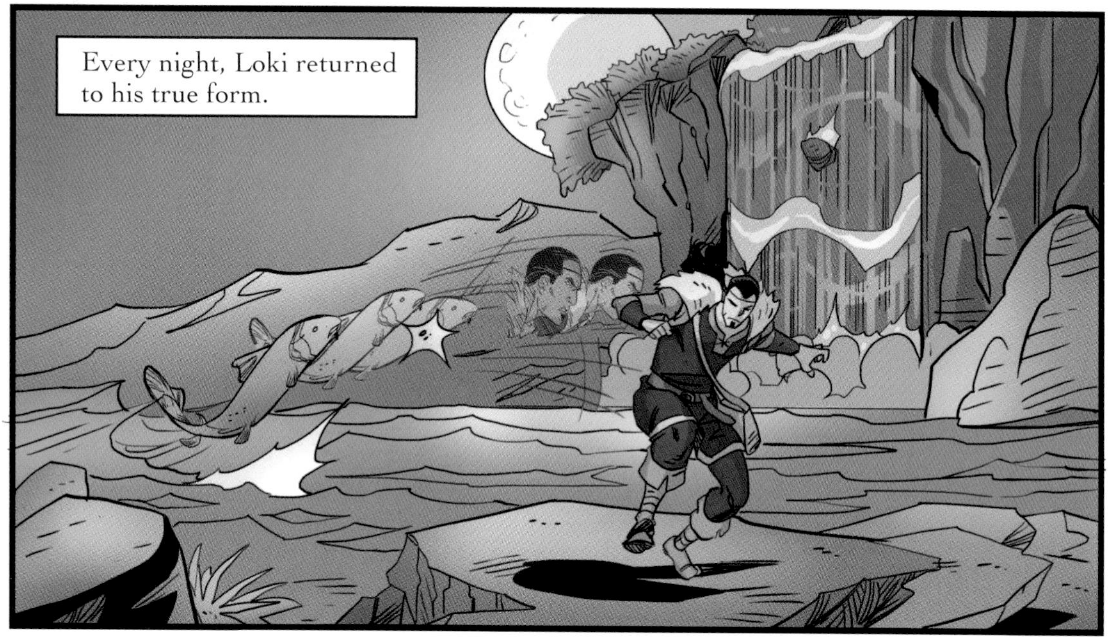
Every night, Loki returned to his true form.

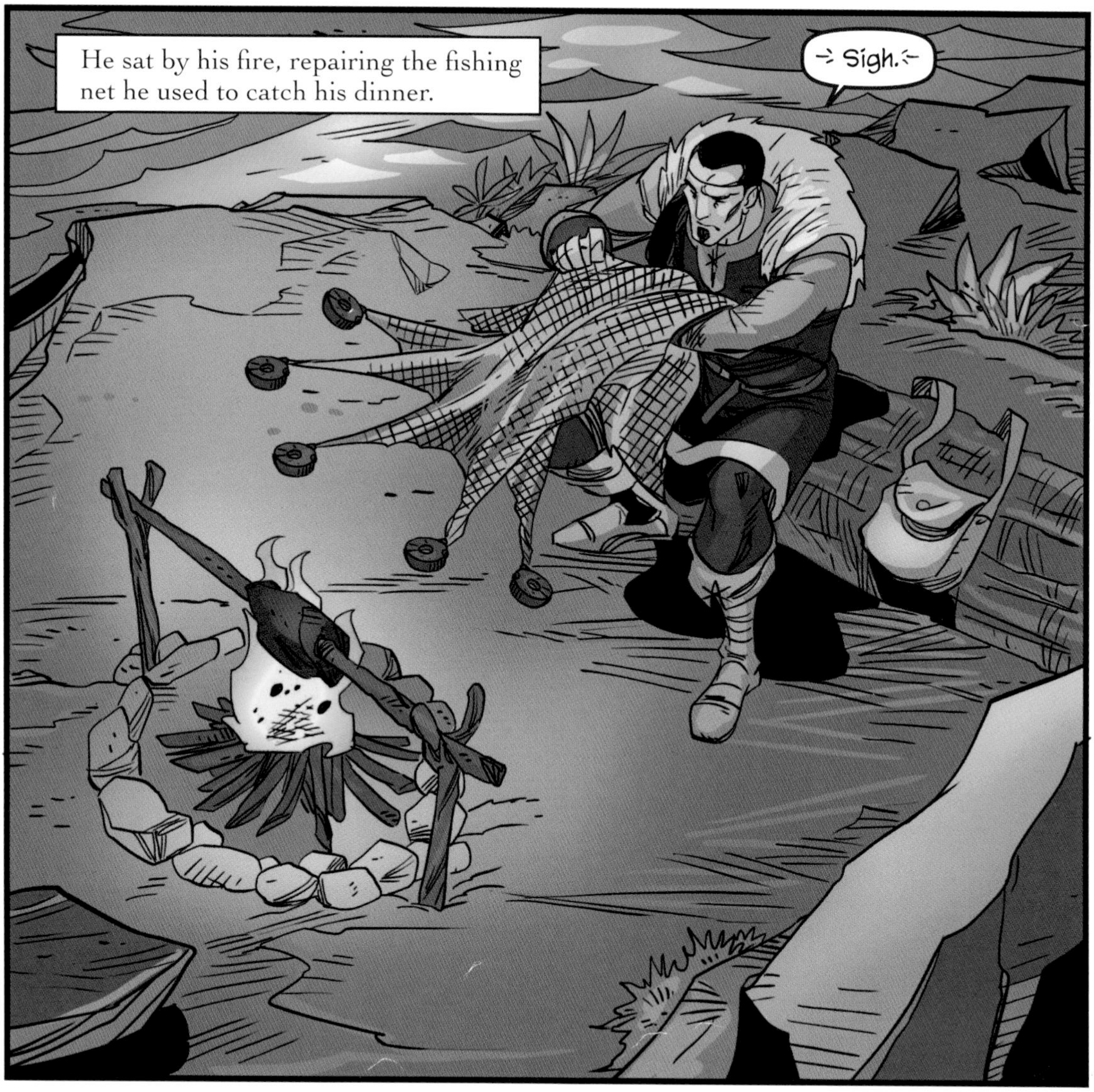
He sat by his fire, repairing the fishing net he used to catch his dinner.
Sigh.

After a while...

Surely they've stopped looking for me by now!

I long to see the *sun* again.

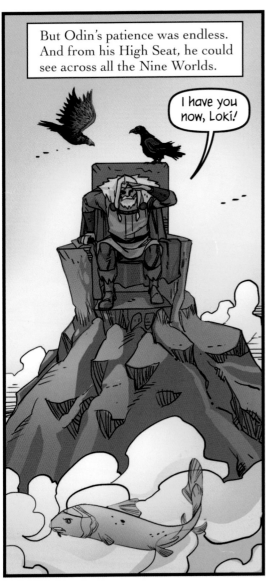

But Odin's patience was endless. And from his High Seat, he could see across all the Nine Worlds.

I have you now, Loki!

Go find Loki! He's beside a stream beyond the *farthest* mountaintop.

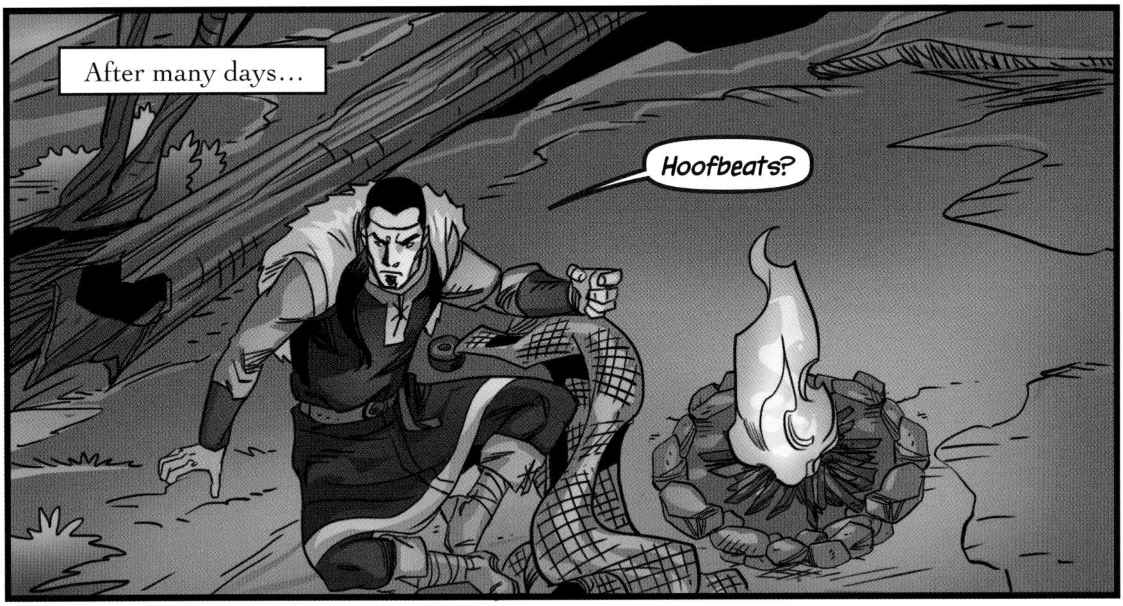
After many days…
Hoofbeats?

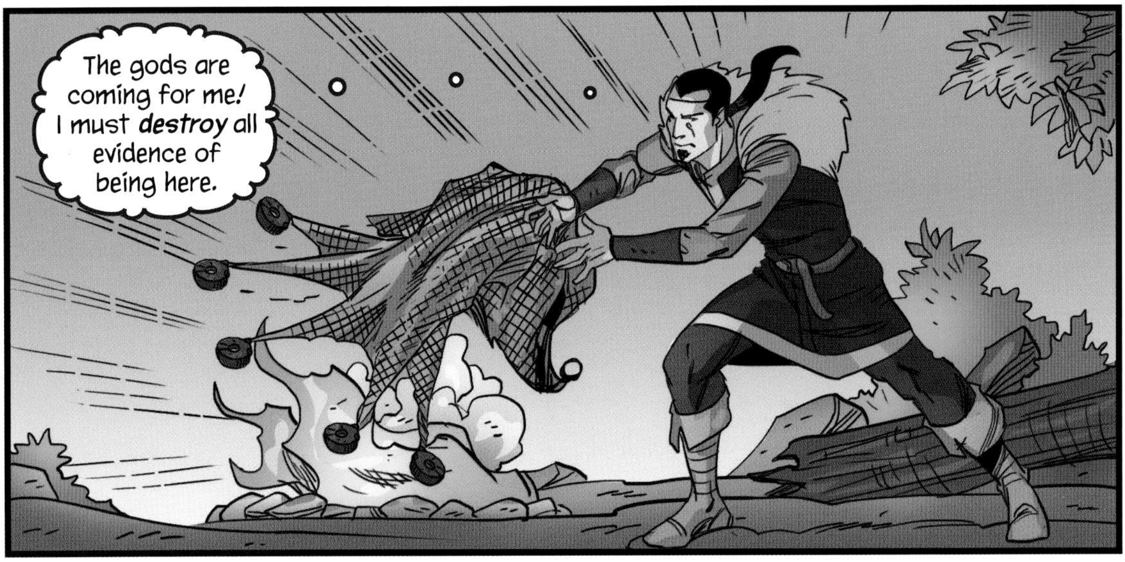
The gods are coming for me! I must *destroy* all evidence of being here.

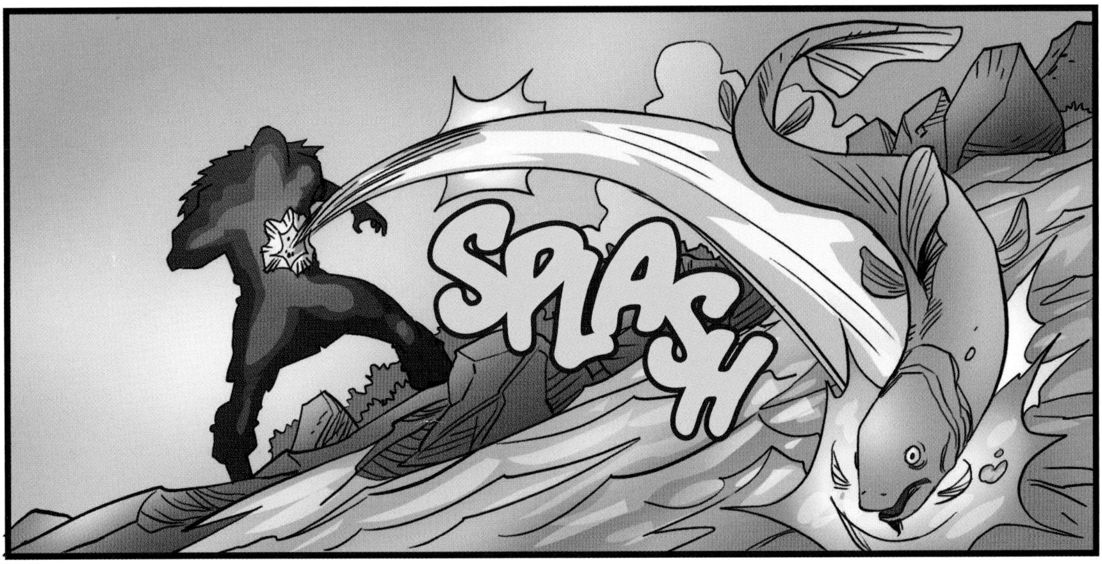
SPLASH

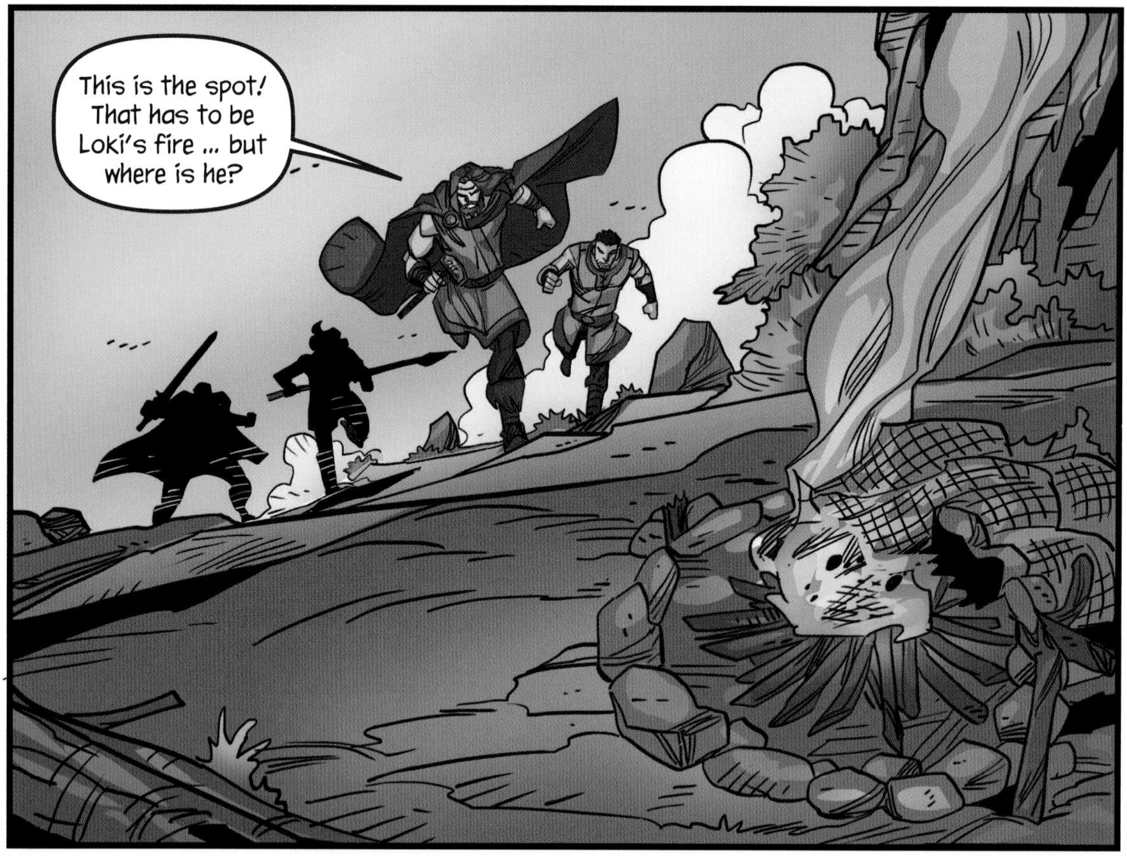
This is the spot! That has to be Loki's fire ... but where is he?

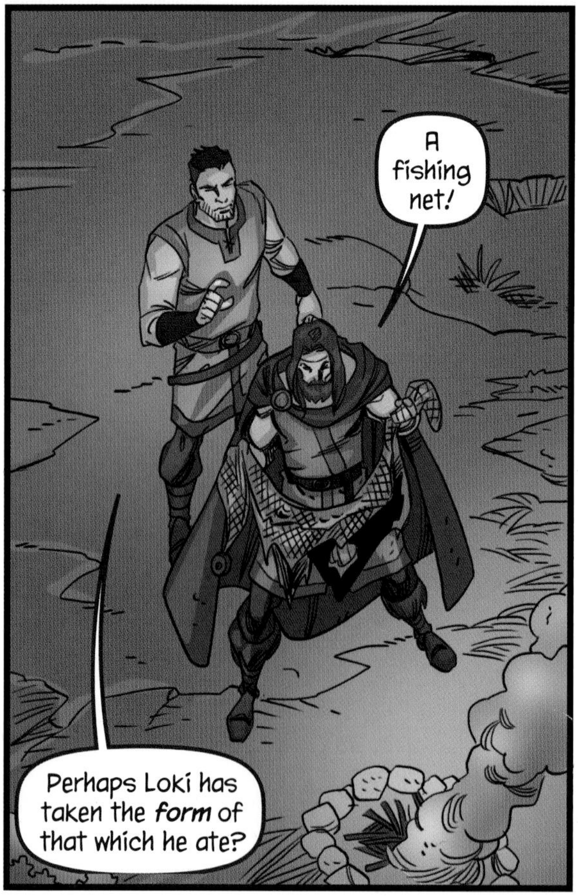
A fishing net!
Perhaps Loki has taken the *form* of that which he ate?

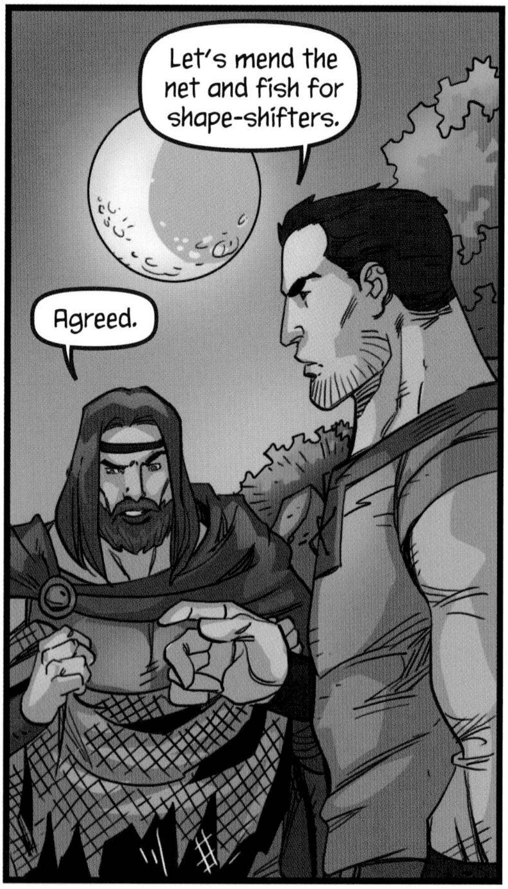
Let's mend the net and fish for shape-shifters.
Agreed.

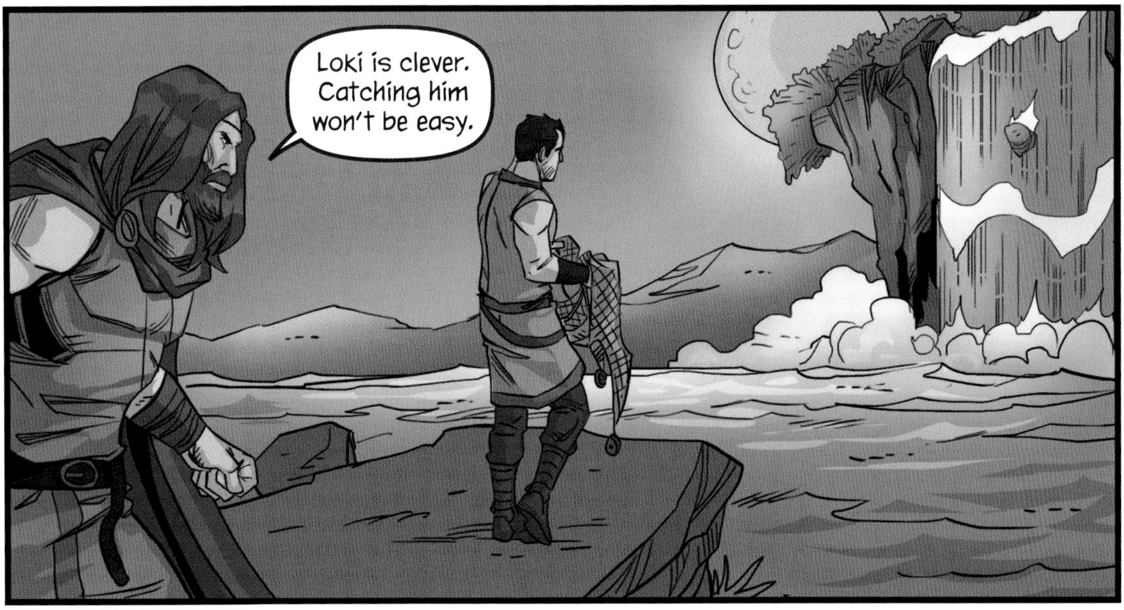
Loki is clever. Catching him won't be easy.

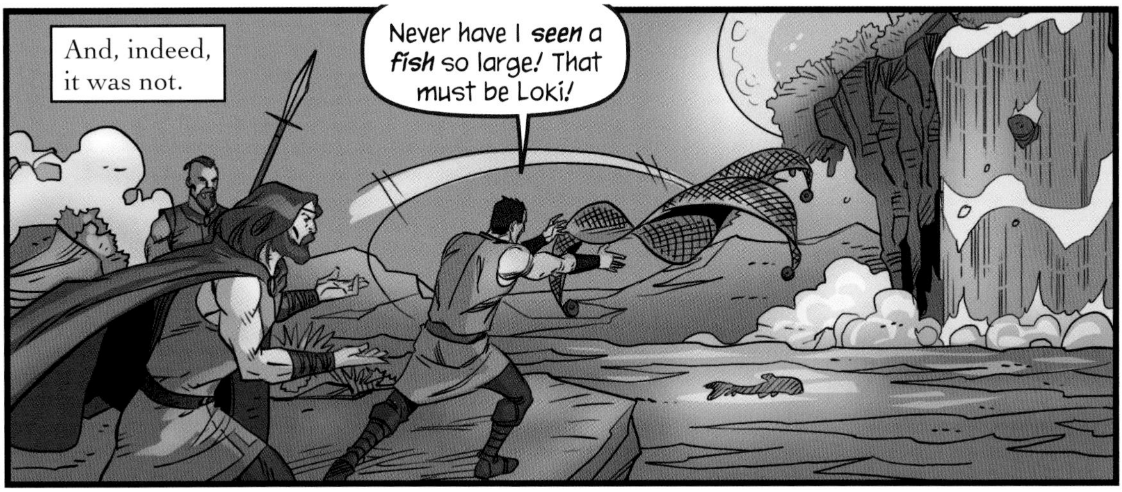
And, indeed, it was not.
Never have I *seen* a *fish* so large! That must be Loki!

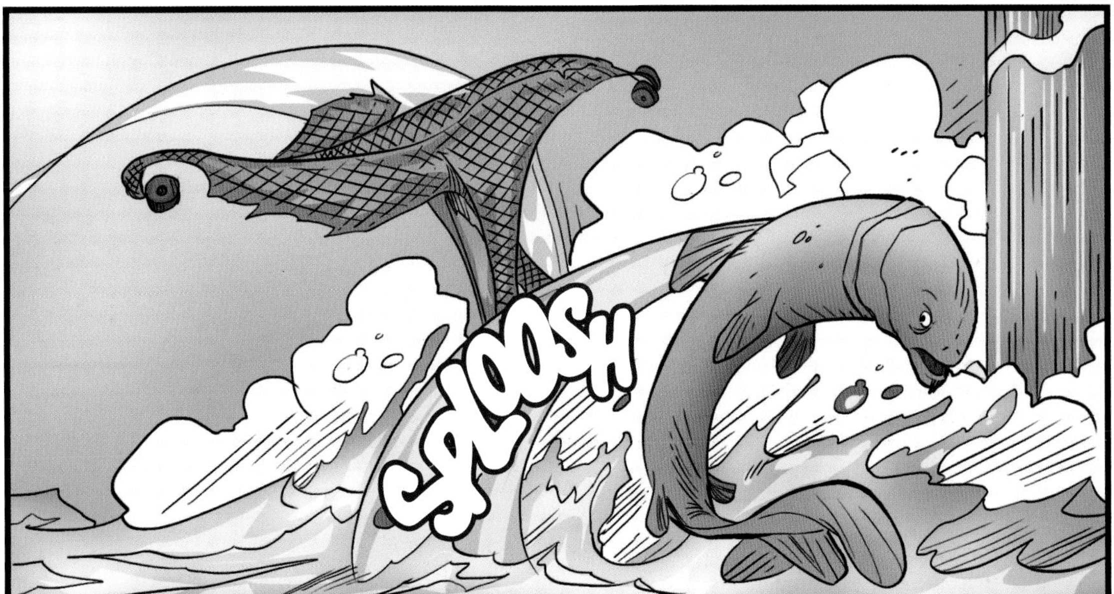
SPLOOSH

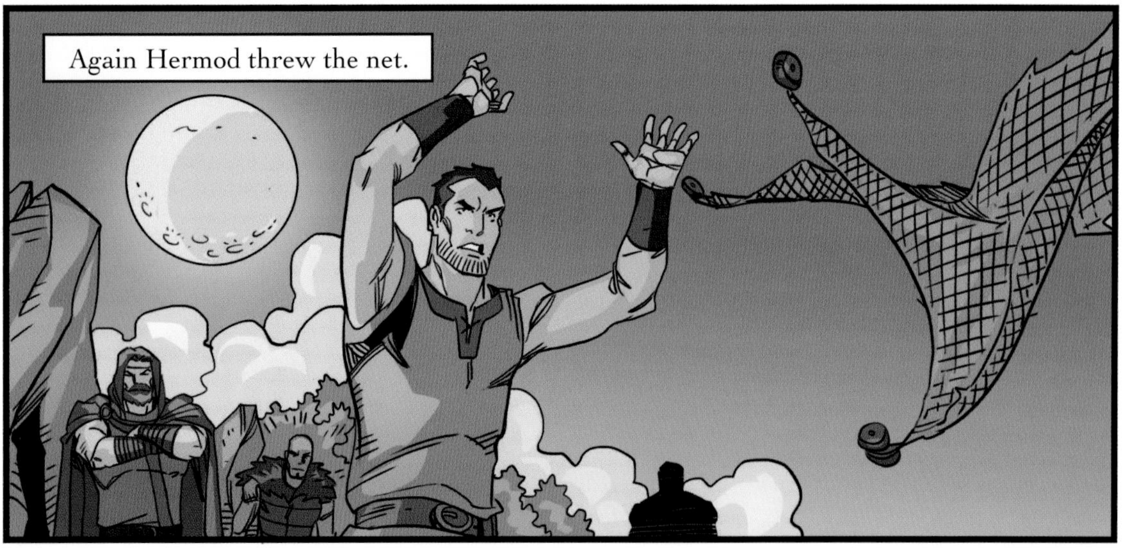
Again Hermod threw the net.

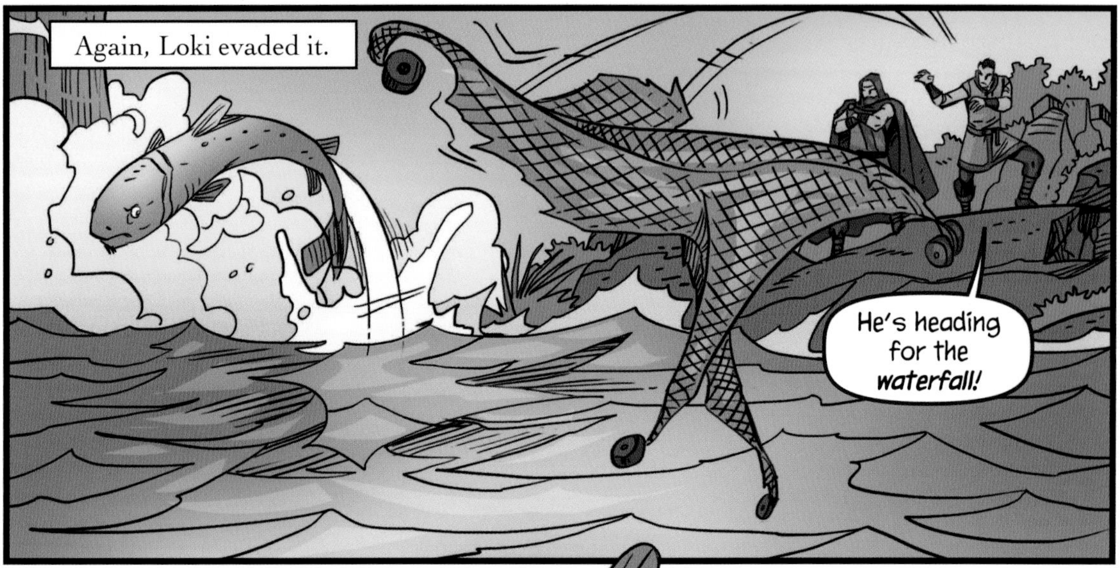
Again, Loki evaded it.
He's heading for the waterfall!

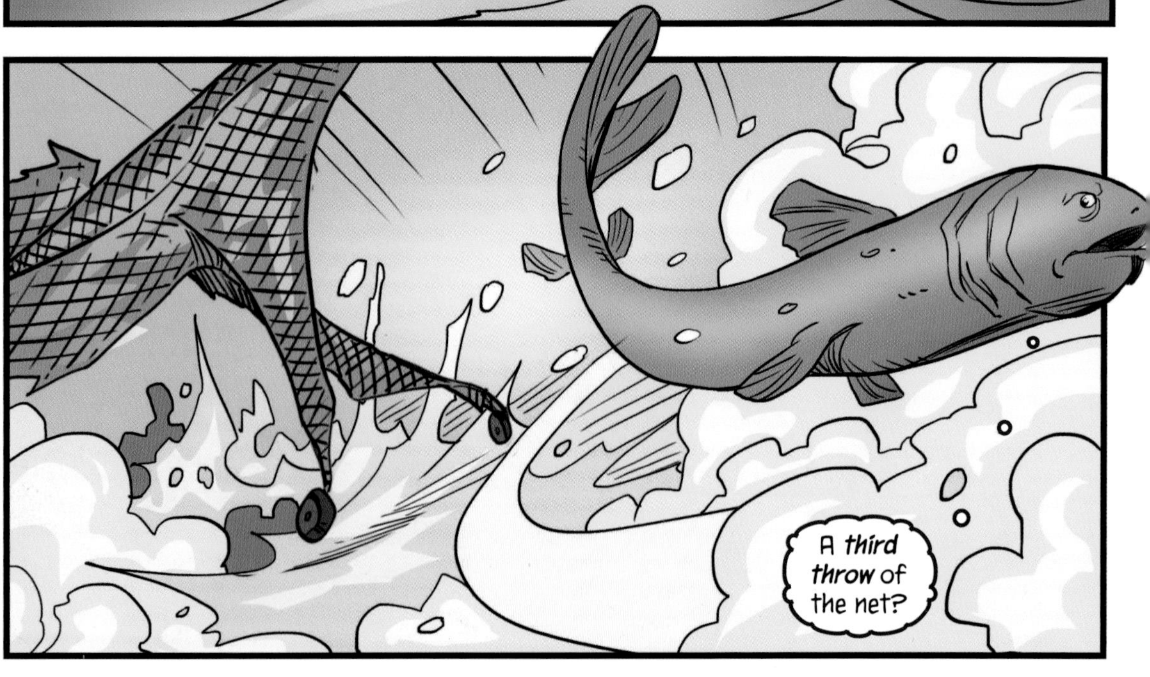
A third throw of the net?

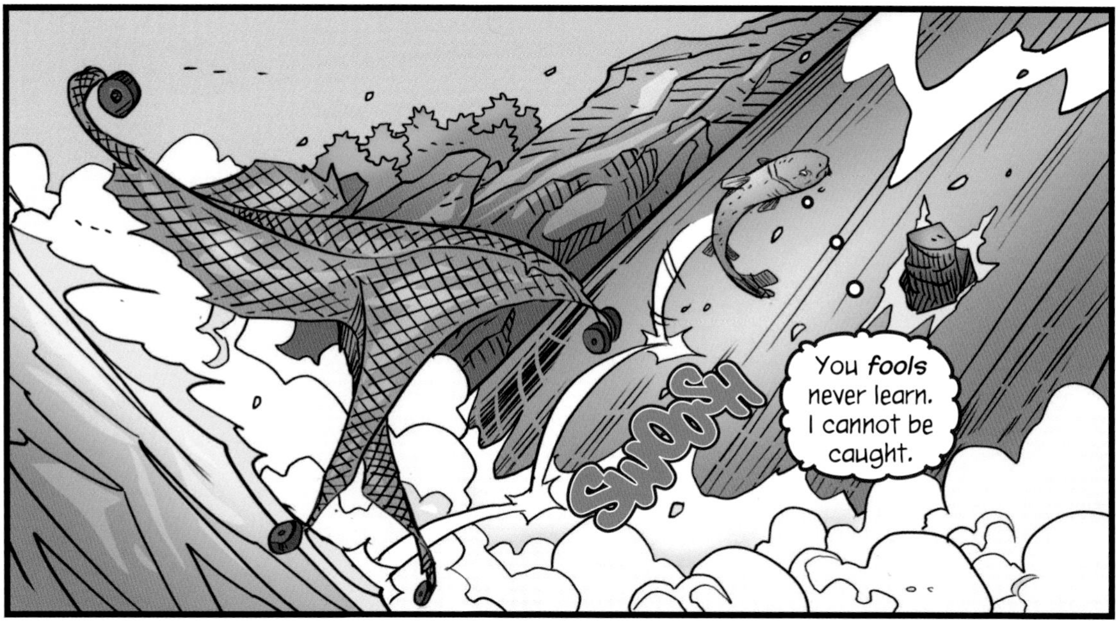
SWOOSH
You *fools* never learn. I cannot be caught.

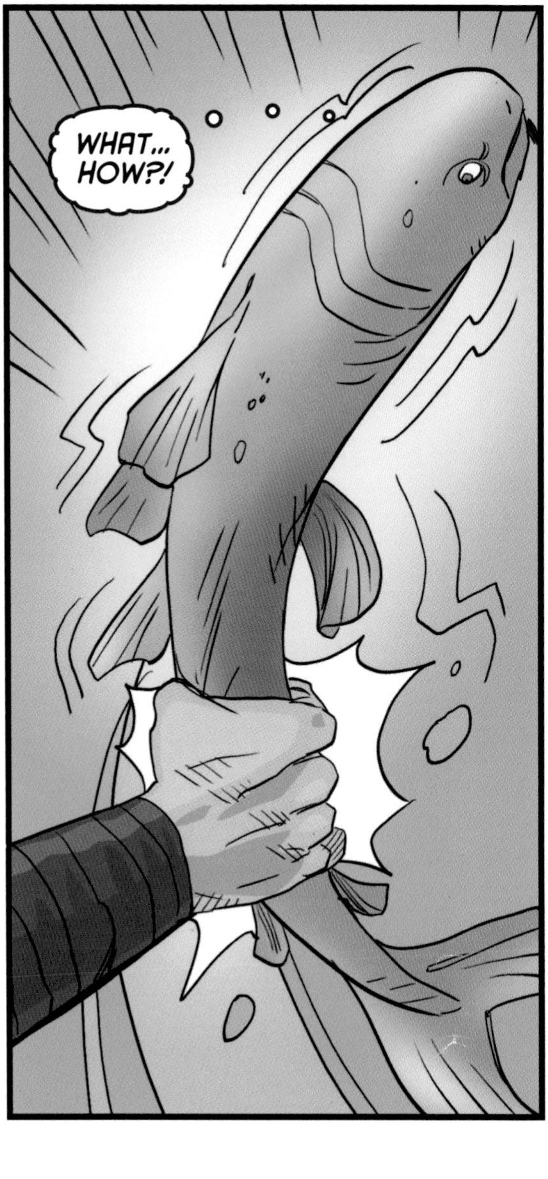
WHAT... HOW?!

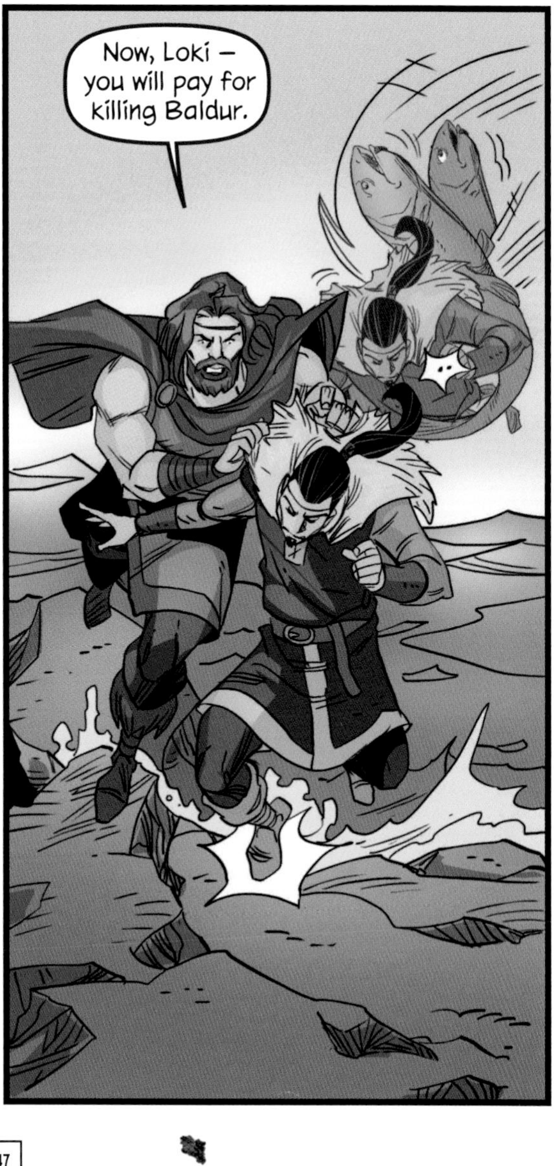
Now, Loki — you will pay for killing Baldur.

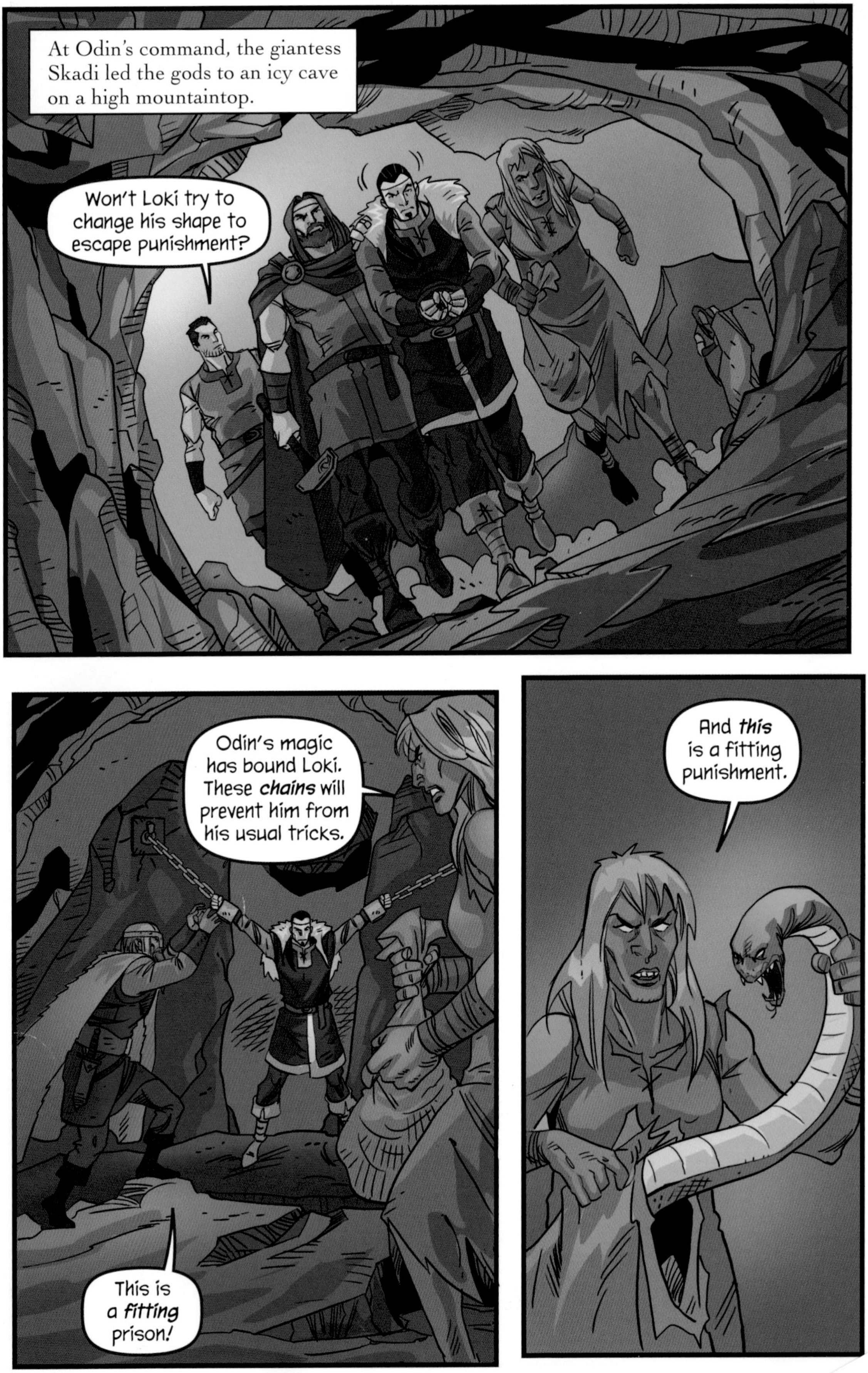
At Odin's command, the giantess Skadi led the gods to an icy cave on a high mountaintop.
Won't Loki try to change his shape to escape punishment?
Odin's magic has bound Loki. These *chains* will prevent him from his usual tricks.
This is a *fitting* prison!
And *this* is a fitting punishment.

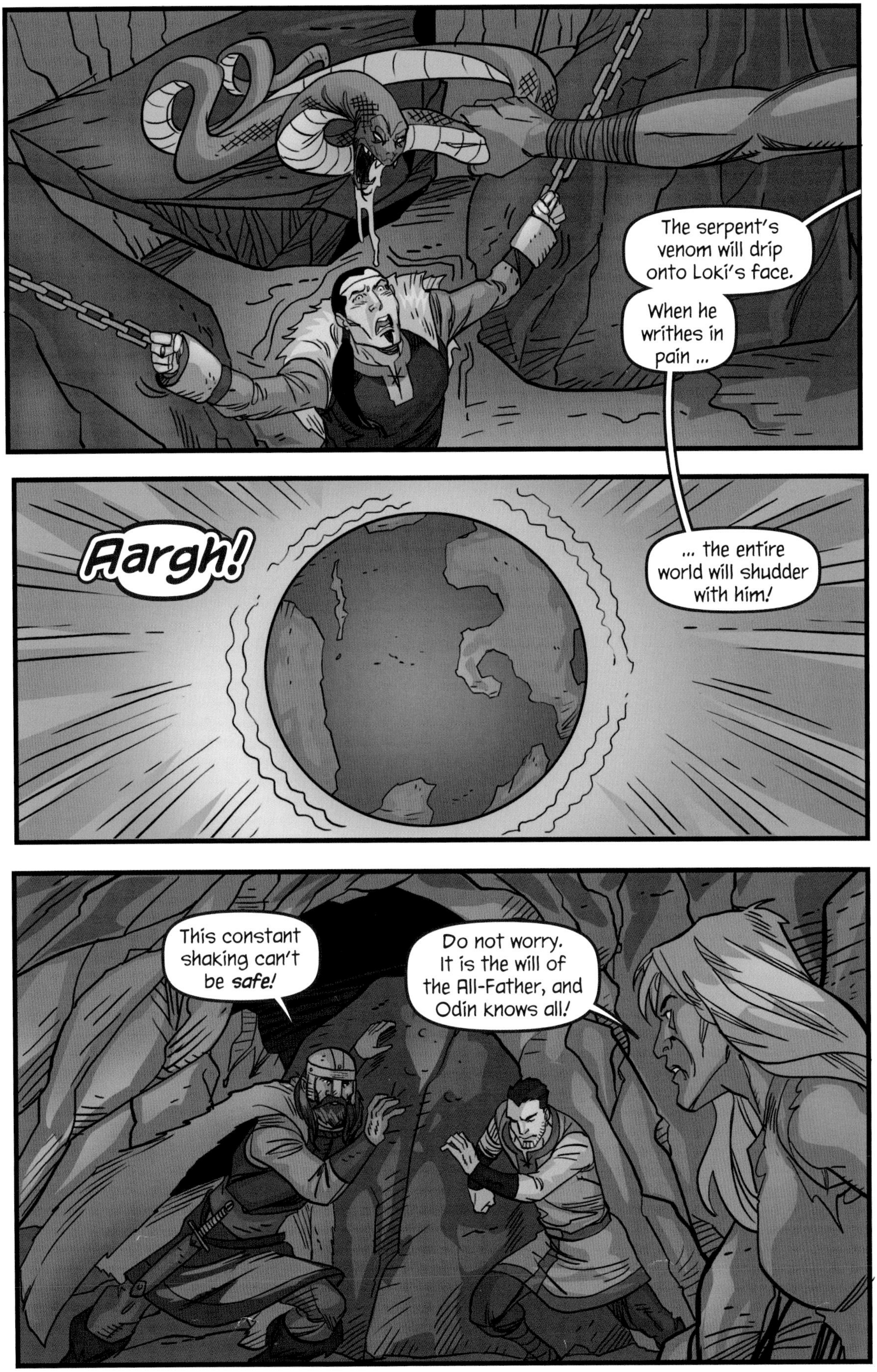

The serpent's venom will drip onto Loki's face.
When he writhes in pain ...
Aargh!
... the entire world will shudder with him!
This constant shaking can't be *safe!*
Do not worry. It is the will of the All-Father, and Odin knows all!

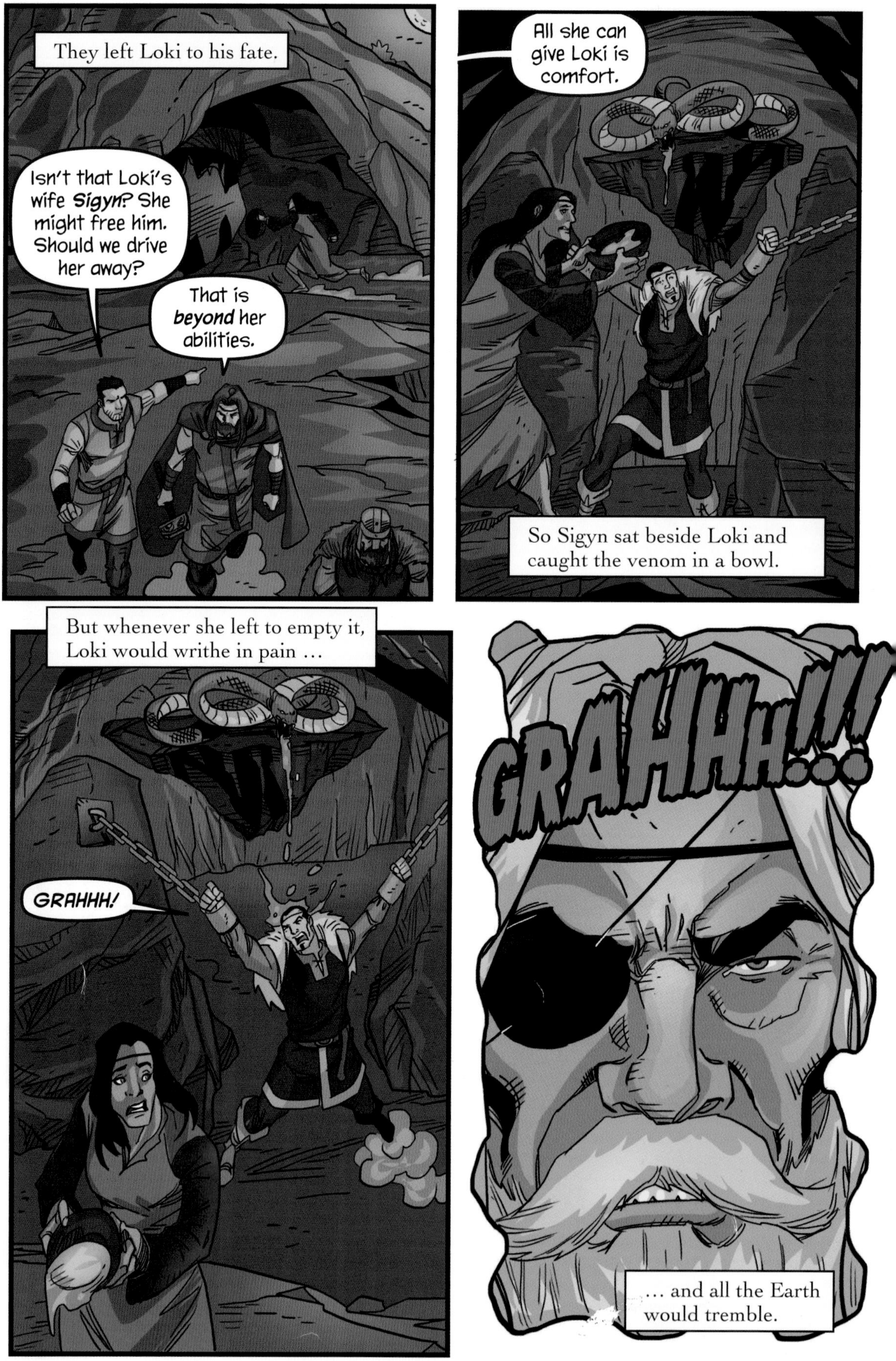
They left Loki to his fate.
Isn't that Loki's wife Sigyn? She might free him. Should we drive her away?
That is beyond her abilities.
All she can give Loki is comfort.
So Sigyn sat beside Loki and caught the venom in a bowl.
But whenever she left to empty it, Loki would writhe in pain …
GRAHHH!
GRAHHH!!!
… and all the Earth would tremble.

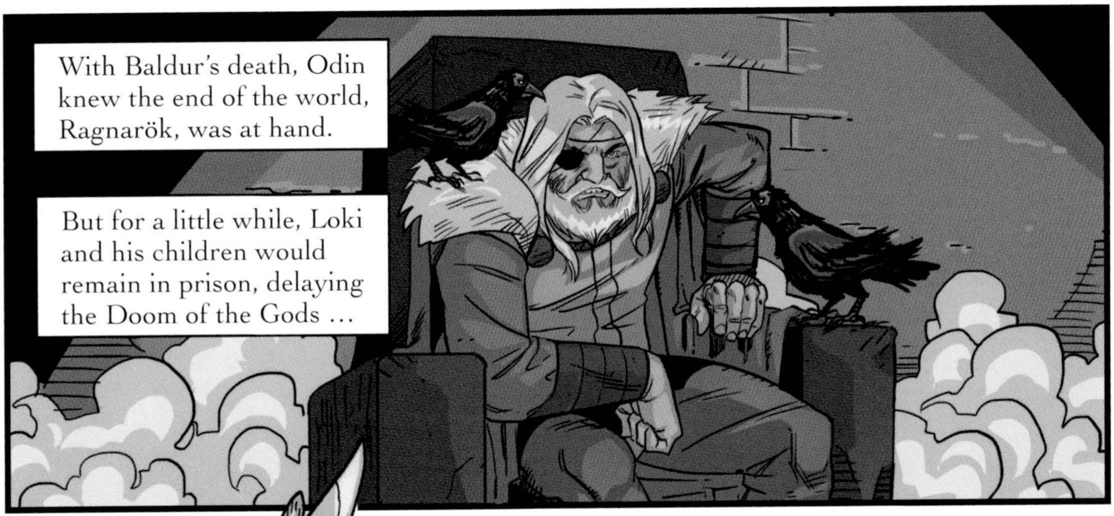
With Baldur's death, Odin knew the end of the world, Ragnarök, was at hand.
But for a little while, Loki and his children would remain in prison, delaying the Doom of the Gods …

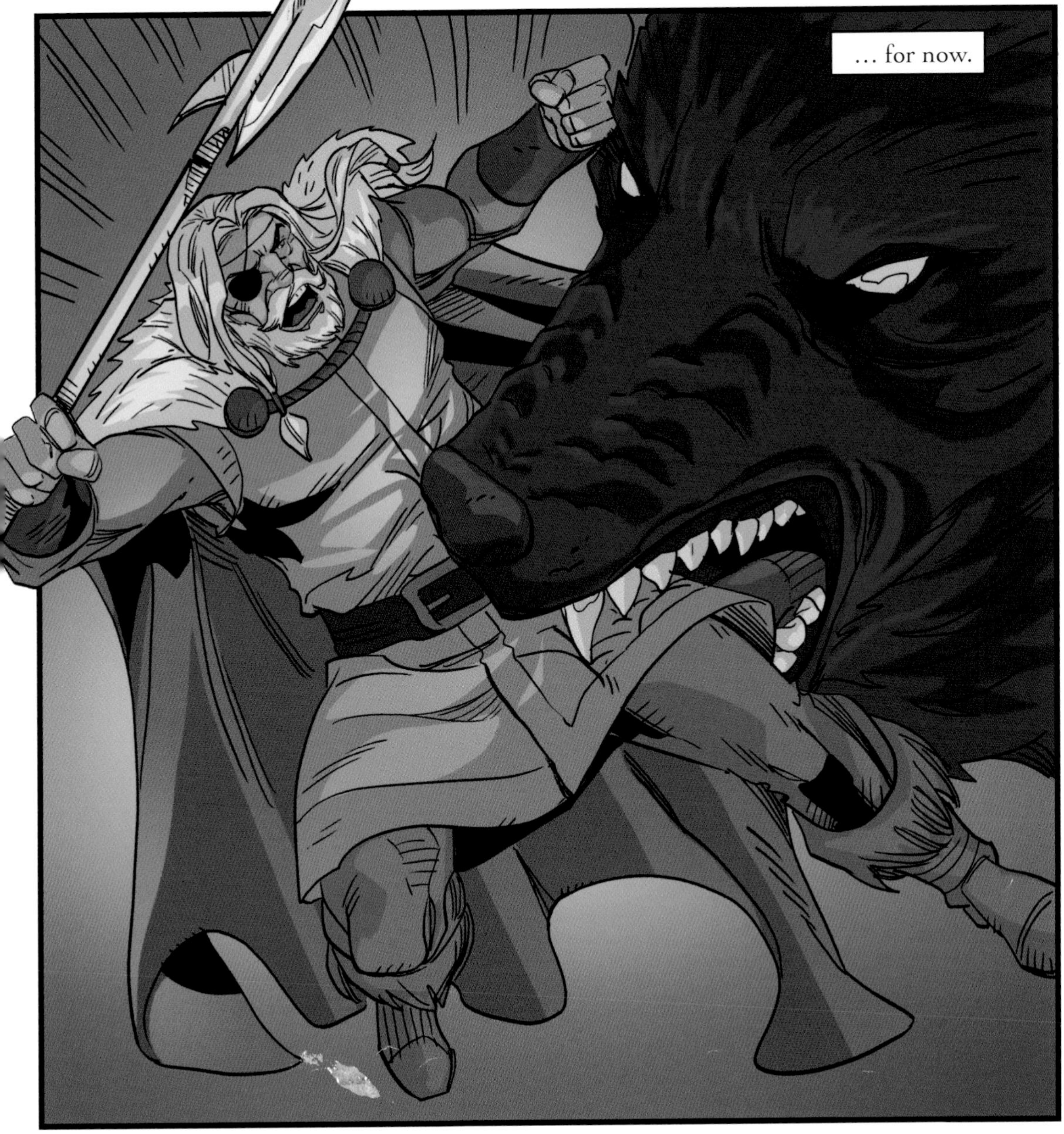
… for now.

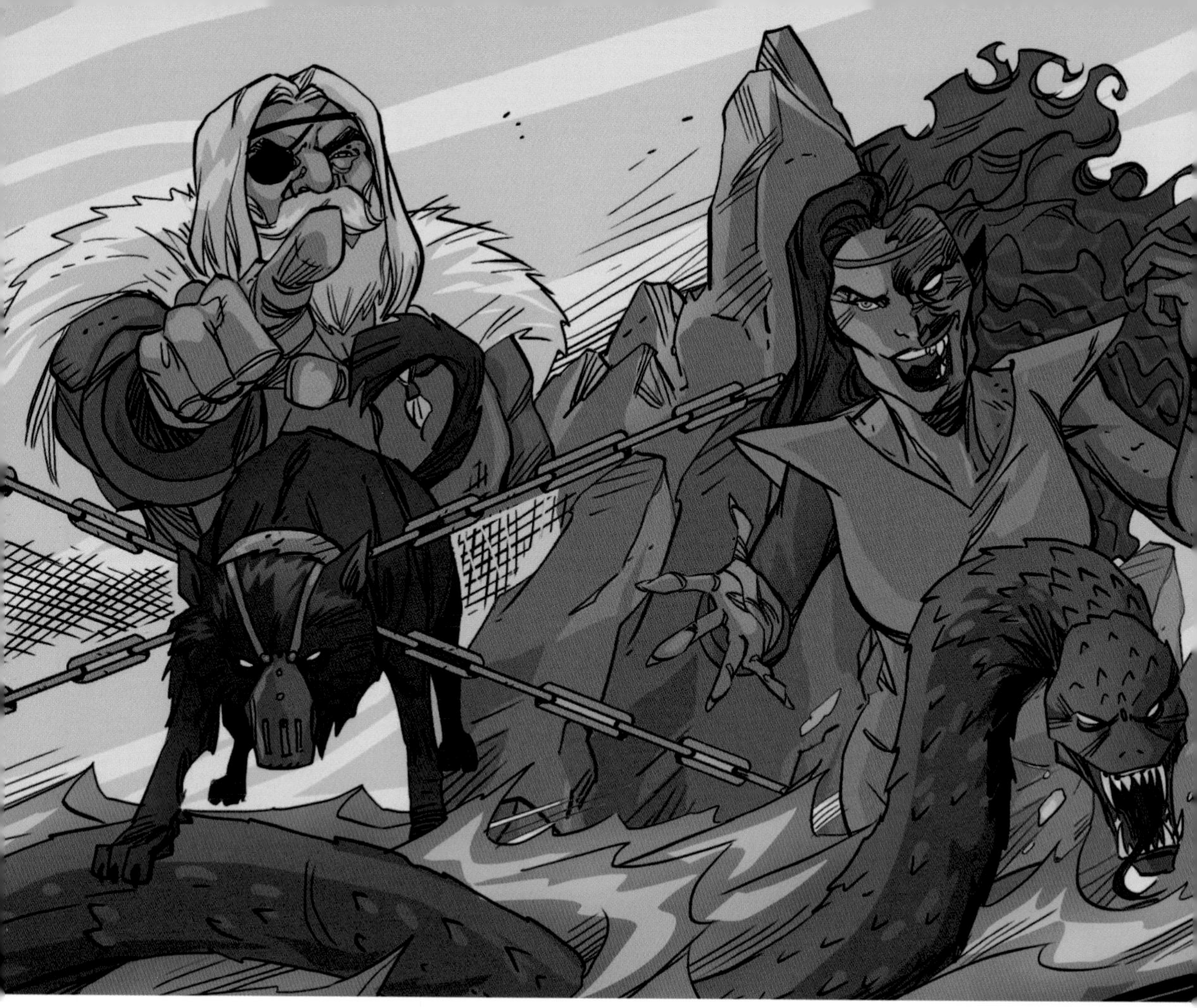

ABOUT THE RETELLING AUTHOR AND ILLUSTRATOR

Louise Simonson enjoys writing about monsters, science fiction, fantasy characters, and superheroes.

She has authored the award-winning Power Pack series, several best-selling X-Men titles, the Web of Spider-Man series for Marvel Comics, and the Superman: Man of Steel series for DC Comics. She has also written many books for kids.

Louise is married to comic artist and writer Walter Simonson and lives in the suburbs of New York City.

Passionate comic book artist **Eduardo Garcia** works from his studio (Red Wolf Studio) in Mexico City with the help of his talented son Sebastian Iñaki. He has brought his talent, pencils, and colors to varied projects for many titles and publishers such as Scooby-Doo (DC Comics), Spiderman Family (Marvel), Flash Gordon (Aberdeen), and Speed Racer (IDW).

GLOSSARY

banquet (BANG-kwit)—a formal meal for a large number of people, usually on a special occasion

evade (i-VADE)—to keep away from someone, or to keep out of someone's way

fate (FAYT)—the supernatural force that some people believe controls events and decides what happens

flattery (FLAT-ur-ee)—excessive or insincere praise of someone to further one's own interests

invulnerable (in-VUHL-nur-uh-buhl)—unable to be harmed

Jötunheim (YOH-toon-heym)—the land of the giants in ancient Norse mythology

microbe (MYE-krobe)—a tiny living thing that is too small to be seen without a microscope

perceptive (pur-SEP-tiv)—able to quickly notice things or understand situations

prophecy (PROF-uh-see)—a prediction

pyre (PYER)—a pile of wood built to burn a dead body for a funeral

seer (SEE-ur)—a person who foretells events

writhe (REYTH)—to twist and turn around, as in pain

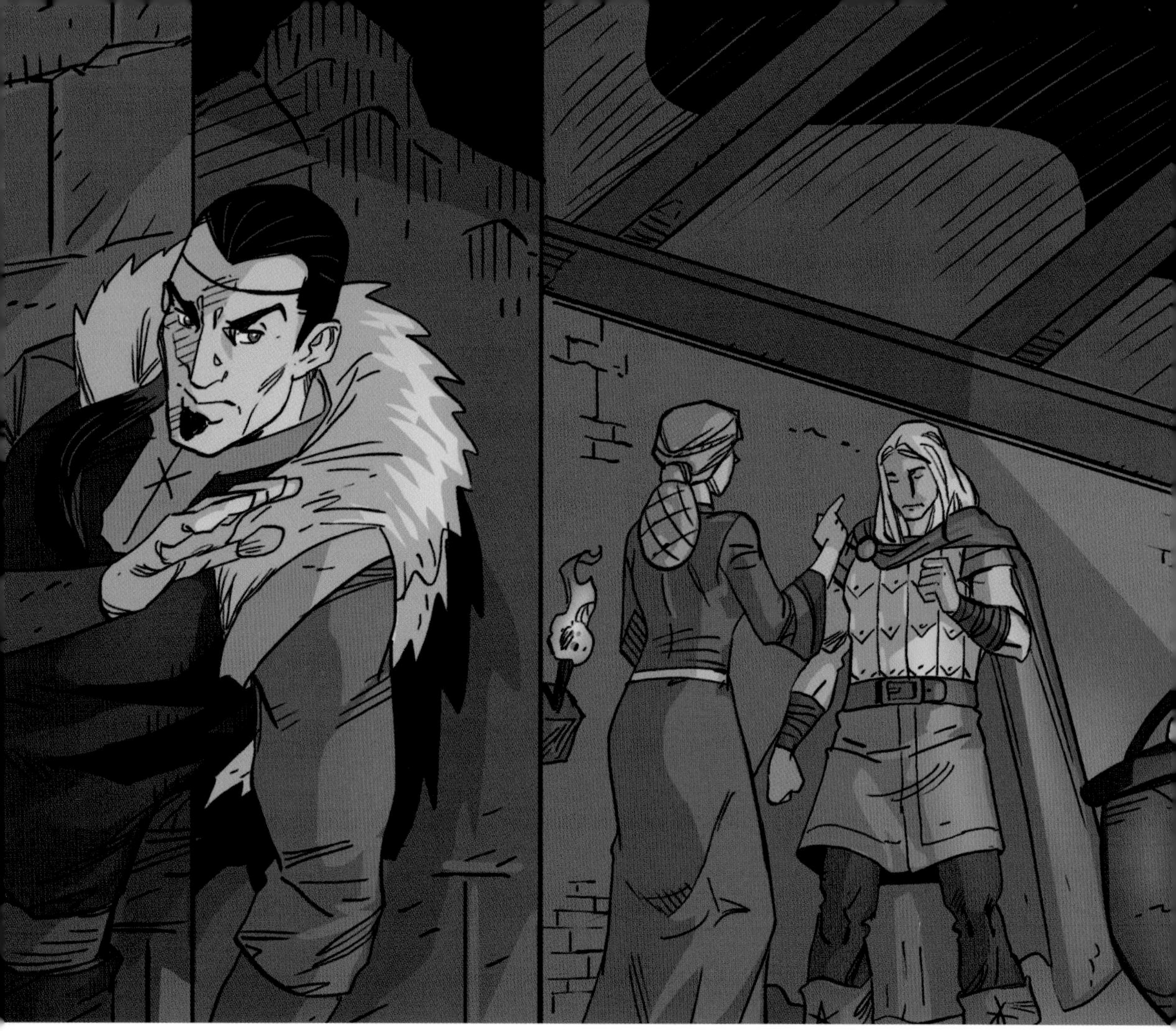

DISCUSSION QUESTIONS

1. Loki used magic and tricks against the Norse gods to bring about the death of Baldur. Why do you think Loki wanted Baldur to die?

2. Baldur's mother, Frigg, convinced everything in the world to help protect her son, except for mistletoe. Why did Frigg think this small plant would not be a threat to Baldur?

3. The ruler of the underworld, Hel, refused to return Baldur to life unless everything in the world wept for him. Why do you think Hel made this demand?

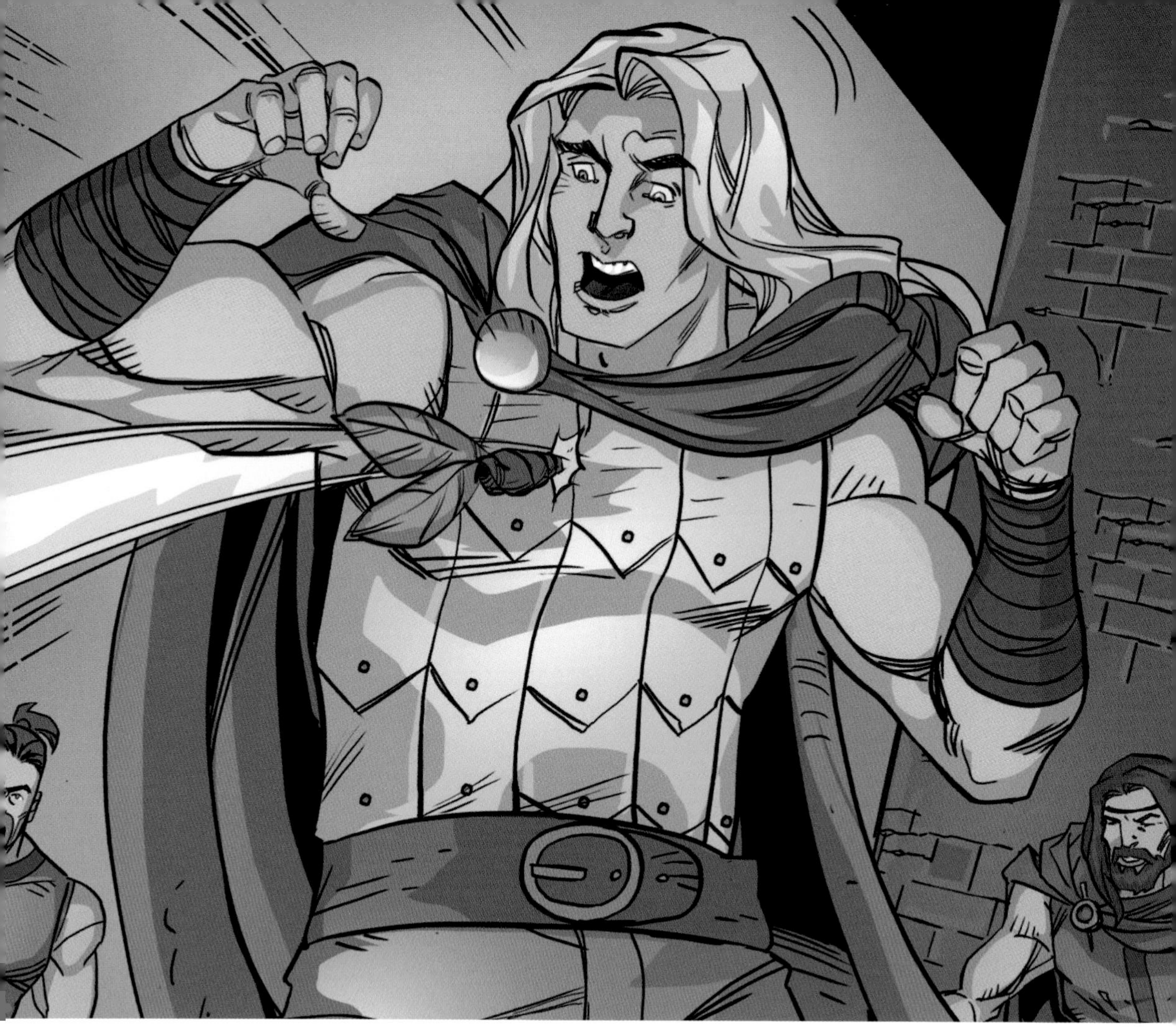

WRITING PROMPTS

1. Baldur had several nightmares about his own death. Have you ever had bad recurring dreams while you sleep? Write down what the dreams were about and what you think they could mean.

2. Loki tricked the blind god Hod into throwing the deadly dart that killed Baldur. Has anyone ever tricked you into doing something that you shouldn't have done? What was the result? Write down what happened and what you could have done differently in that situation.

3. When Loki became a fish, the other gods tried and failed to catch him with a net. What do you think they could have done instead? Write down how you would catch Loki if you were a Norse god.

READ THEM ALL!

NORSE
MYTHS
A VIKING GRAPHIC NOVEL
THOR AND LOKI
by BOWEN and SMITH and LOKUS

NORSE
MYTHS
A VIKING GRAPHIC NOVEL
THOR VS. THE GIANTS
by BOWEN and GARCIA

NORSE
MYTHS
A VIKING GRAPHIC NOVEL
THE DEATH OF BALDUR
by SIMONSON and GARCIA

NORSE
MYTHS
A VIKING GRAPHIC NOVEL
TWILIGHT OF THE GODS
by DAHL and GARCIA

ONLY FROM STONE ARCH BOOKS!

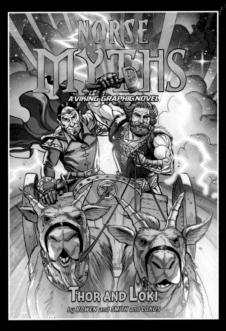

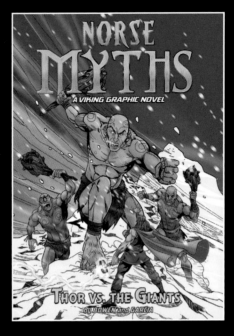

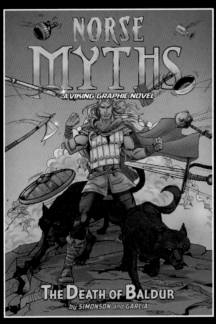

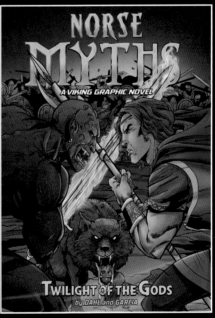